HELLO, FUTURE ME

kim Ventrella

Scholastic Press
New York

Library of Congress Cataloging-in-Publication Data available

ISBN 978-1-338-57617-7

10 9 8 7 6 5 4 3 2 1   20 21 22 23 24

Printed in the U.S.A.   23

First edition, August 2020

Book design by Yaffa Jaskoll

To Past and Future Me:
Don't worry, kid,
you got this!

TO: ladyvangogh7@gmail.com
FROM: juniepiethegreat@gmail.com
SUBJECT: Can't wait to see you!

Mom! Can you believe it's been five weeks? I can, because it's felt like forever. Last night, Dad said we had to do all the laundry before you got home, and do you know how long it takes to do five weeks' worth of laundry? Basically, forever. But it's a good thing we did, because the house smells a lot better now, so yay!

Dad also said we could bake something special for when you get here, since it's my twelfth birthday! Not that we're having an awesome joint party or anything, just a totally laid-back dessert. Anyway, I said, "Are you sure you know how to bake?" And he told me how cake mixes have recipes right on the back of the boxes, so how hard could it be? But it turns out, pretty hard. We didn't make a cake so much as a flat chocolate pancake. Sorry!

After that, I said we should order a fancy cake from Sasquatch Sweeties, on account of our double celebration, but did you know that fancy cakes cost $54.99? And that's just for the square ones, not the ones made in special shapes. I wanted to get you a cake decorated like Vincent van Gogh's *The Starry Night*, since that's your favorite painting, but Mrs. Emme, as in Mrs. Emmeline Sweetie, said that if she could paint like Van Gogh, then she wouldn't be stuck here in Tanglewood Crossing talking to me, now would she? Then she gave me and Dad a scoop of frosting on the house, probably because she knew Dad couldn't afford to pay $54.99 for some boring square cake.

All that to say, we ended up getting you a bag of your favorite strawberry-flavored Twizzlers, which may not seem that great, but, just so you know, we tried. Dad especially.

I hope you learned a lot at adult art camp—who even knew they had camps for adults—and also that you had "time to think," since that's why you wanted to go in the first place. It seems like you could think just about anywhere, like even in Tanglewood Crossing, but then again I don't know a lot about art.

Ooh, I almost forgot! I have news. You know how you called me a matchmaker, because I'm the reason Merline and Big Vic finally fell in love? Well, I got Coach Mitch a date! It's true! Do you remember Coach Mitch?

He's the coach of Calvin's soccer team. Anyway, Dad and I were in the stands watching a game, and I noticed how Coach Mitch kept laughing whenever the new assistant coach, Miss Richards, said anything, like even really boring stuff like what type of detergent they should use on their new uniforms. Then I asked in my loudest voice if Coach Mitch was going to the Bigfoot Ball, because I know from my top secret sources that Miss Richards loves dancing, and he said he would love to go but that he didn't have a date. So, I said what about Miss Richards, and Coach Mitch turned so red his head almost exploded—not a joke—but then Miss Richards said she'd love to go, and now it's a date.

I guess you were right, I really am a matchmaker. That just goes to show that you can do anything if you really put your mind to it. Even make two people fall in love!

Did I mention I can't wait till you get home?!? Which . . . drumroll, please . . . happens in about three hours! Spoiler alert, Calvin is helping me make an epic "Welcome Home" sign so you can find us at the airport. It involves a lot of glitter. As in A LOT! You can't miss it.

Dad says we'll meet you at baggage claim and then

we'll head straight home for . . . second drumroll . . . a
surprise! Can't wait to hear all about camp.
See you soon, as in REALLY SOON!
Love,
June

June's Extra-Thick Planning Notebook, p. 323
Mom's Coming Home Checklist

- Do laundry (check)

- Buy special dessert (check)

- Make epic "Welcome Home" sign (almost check)

- Plan super-secret birthday/welcome home party (check)

- Pick up Mom's gift (DON'T FORGET!!!)

CHAPTER 1

RUINED!

Most legends start with an adventurer setting
out on some epic quest. This story starts with a sequin in
my eyeball, courtesy of my best friend and super-annoying
person, Calvin. As beginnings go, it may not seem that exciting, but it sure as heck hurt.

"Sorry, I was aiming for your mouth," Calvin said as I
picked the offending sequin out of my eye socket.

"Uck, it's covered in eye goo. Look."

"Yeah, that happens."

I crushed the sequin between my fingers and glared, but
Calvin being Calvin, I couldn't stay mad. It's basically a

superpower. No matter what he does, he has this way of making you forgive him for everything ever, no matter what. Mom says it's in the eyes—and I don't mean like a sequin in the eyes, but a feeling. Then again, Mom's an artist, so she says a lot of stuff about feelings I don't understand. When she looks around, she's not looking at the boring, regular world like you and me. I mean, she is, but to her boring stuff looks extra beautiful and full of meaning.

Anyway, this one time she tried to draw Calvin's eyes, which are brown and deep and kind of sad, but she could never get them right, because according to her some people carry around their feelings in their eyes. Apparently, eye feelings are something you can't capture in paint.

"How does that look?" Calvin said, holding up the WELCOME HOME sign we'd spent the last hour decorating. In that moment, sitting in our favorite booth in The Friendly Bean, sun beams shining in through the front window making all that glittery stuff sparkle like stars, that sign was the most beautiful sight in the whole wide world. Even more so because it meant that Mom was finally coming home.

"We might not be artists, but I'd say this baby's sheer perfection," Calvin added with one of his irritating smiles. Irritating because I was trying my best to stay in angry mode—hello, eye sequin!—but I had no choice but to agree.

After that, we settled into our usual routine, enjoying half a Jelly Belly donut apiece, Merline's specialty, and Sasquatch Smoothies on the house, thanks to Big Vic. To get you up to speed, Merline and Big Vic own The Friendly Bean, the best and only coffee shop in Tanglewood Crossing, and it's located in our famous downtown, nestled next to a dozen other shops, all in colorful storefronts stacked one on top of the other like presents.

My favorite shops are Wild Man Books, Bigfoot Burger, Heavenly Scoops, and A Yeti Sits Down for Tea, because tea is fancy and tastes really good once you try it. As you can tell, most of the shops here are bigfoot themed, since that is Tanglewood Crossing's main claim to fame. We're home to more bigfoot sightings than any other place in the country, according to Dr. Eliza Day, aka Gram, and she's never wrong.

Gram is the whole reason that everyone in Tanglewood Crossing loves bigfoot, me included. She's a world-famous researcher, or at least she was until she broke her hip hiking the Ouachita Mountains. Now she spends her days cooped up in the Shady Pines nursing home, waiting for her hip to heal. Last week, she said she might have to quit bigfoot hunting for good.

That's why Calvin and I want to make a real bigfoot discovery this year. Something rock-solid, like a hair sample or maybe a piece of poop. That way, Gram will have to stop being sad and get back to hunting. That's the plan anyway.

I have a lot of plans, in case you can't tell.

"Looks like you're ready to celebrate," Big Vic said, coming over to admire our sign, which was clearly a true work of art. Here's a little more about Big Vic. He looks kind of like Gimli from *The Lord of the Rings*, except he's super tall and his beard is all gray. "Why don't you and your mom stop by tomorrow? I'll give you a Heartbreaker Special, on the house."

"You stop giving away all my food," Merline called over from her perch. She was currently balancing atop a ladder, hanging up shiny red bigfoot cupids to go with her streamers and fuzzy hearts. Merline was by far the coolest old lady I'd ever met, with her buzz cut, tongue ring, and super-scary eyebrows. I definitely wanted to be just like her when I grew up.

"I'll agree to stop giving away freebies if you come down here and give me a kiss."

"Here we go." Calvin pretended to gag into his smoothie. "This is all your fault, you know."

"Sorry," I said, but I couldn't argue. Technically, Merline and Big Vic being lovey-dovey all the time was my fault, since I was the one who got them together. To be fair, it hadn't taken much persuading, but it had still cemented my status, at least according to Mom, as Tanglewood Crossing's premier matchmaker.

Merline screwed up her mouth, eyeing Big Vic with her famous icy cold stare. As someone who's known her since forever, I could tell it was just a show. "The day I kiss you, Victor Hudgins, will be the day bigfoot strolls in and orders up a latte."

Big Vic laughed, that kind of deep, rumbling laugh that made his whole belly shake, and he went over and gave Merline a slobbery smooch.

"Shouldn't there be laws against that sort of thing?" Calvin said, grimacing.

"Look away, my friend. Look away," I advised.

Calvin focused on sipping his smoothie, and I sat back, admiring the sight of sunbeams twinkling on the world's most beautiful sign.

"You know," Calvin said, after Big Vic headed off to help a group of tourists in jean shorts and fanny packs, "it's almost time for the Bigfoot Ball."

"Yup, hence all the sparkly decorations," I said, but I was only half listening. My brain was wrapped up in thoughts of Mom coming home. I scanned my to-do list again. The only thing left was to finish this piece of true and utter beauty, and then pick up Mom's gift.

"June?" Calvin said, clearing his throat. "Can I ask you something?"

"Sure," I said. Again, not much with the active listening.

"It's about the Bigfoot Ball."

"Okay, but first hold up that sign. I want one last look before— Yikes! Is that the time? We've got to go!"

I gave the sign one final glance before rolling it up, very carefully, and sliding a rubber band around the outside. Boy oh boy, was it a beaut! "This'll have to do. It's officially go time. Get your stuff, and let's head out! I still have to pick up Mom's gift!"

"What? Now?" Calvin said, looking more flustered than usual. "I thought we still had a few minutes. I wanted to ask you about . . . um . . . never mind."

"You can ask me later, okay? There's no time!" My hands flew, stuffing glitter and scissors and markers into my bag. "This gift is the most important part of Mom's

Welcome Home Extravaganza. Without it, everything will be ruined."

"I'm coming. But I didn't finish my drink."

"No buts! I don't want Mom to think that we're only celebrating my birthday. This is her day too, and she needs the perfect gift."

Calvin tried to chug the last of his smoothie, but I snagged him by the sleeve and pulled him toward the door.

"Okay, I'm coming already," Calvin said, bending down to tie his shoe.

I explained how I'd make it up to him if he'd just hurry, and how Mom's gift had to be absolutely freaking perfect, because if it wasn't, then the whole surprise party/birthday would be officially ruined, and I would be forced to crawl into a cave somewhere and starve to death.

"At least you're not being dramatic about it," Calvin said, which was another one of those times when he was being super annoying, but I didn't even get mad about it. Like I said, he has a superpower.

"Just hurry up, pleeease," I said, strangling the door handle.

"Sigh, fine. Where is this place anyway?"

"You've never been to Mountain Musings? It's the only

place in like a million miles with decent art supplies!" I said, with zero drama in my voice.

Calvin laughed. "Whatever, lead the way."

Mountain Musings was actually awesome, even for a total nonartist like me. Inside, the walls were covered in murals of Tanglewood Crossing, including twenty-seven hidden bigfoots. Seriously, I counted once. Looking around at the walls was kind of like playing the world's biggest game of Where's Waldo, except with a lot more hair and fewer stripes. It was also the place Mom liked to hang out most, when she wasn't painting in her closet/art studio, taking one of her long walks in the woods for "inspiration," or Skyping with her old friends in New York, where Mom is from.

Finally, Calvin finished tying his shoe, and we stepped outside into a wall of muggy heat. Seriously, within ten seconds of hurrying down that hot, cobbled street, I could taste sweat dripping into my mouth. To our left, we saw one of the big yellow bigfoot buses that stop in town twice a day to pick up tourists and drive them deep into Tanglewood Forest. They're pretty hard to miss because of the color and the giant hairy foot perched on top. To our right, Main Street curved around to form a semicircle of shops, like something straight out of Diagon Alley, except you won't find any wand shops or pubs with magic brick walls—trust me, I've checked.

Even though I've lived here all my life, the tiny downtown with its cobbled streets and old-fashioned oil lamps still fills me with wonder, like I'm walking into a fairy tale. Except it's mostly tourists and overflowing trash cans and a pee smell that never goes away, but still . . . magical.

I led the way around the bend, Calvin wiping his face with the inside of his shirt, and stopped at the opening to a narrow alleyway. I could hear barking from the pet shop on my right, and squealing from the day care on my left, but the alley stood dark and silent.

"You first," Calvin said. So. Rude. But I let it drop. This was gift time. One final check on my list, and this would officially be the best day ever. Mom was coming home. Which meant that the thing she'd needed five weeks to "think" about couldn't have been that important after all. Right? Pretty soon, it would be me and Mom and Dad, back together again, just like on my vision board, and just in time for my birthday!

I stepped from the sunlight into the shade of the alley. A chill wind swept past, despite the heat, sending prickles up my skin. The cobbles angled down, becoming almost like stairs, and I had to bend my knees to keep from falling forward.

"Come on," I said, tugging on Calvin's sleeve to make him follow.

There were no other shops down here, and we only passed one other door, a large, elaborately carved one that had been painted a shocking shade of pink.

"Let's hurry up," Calvin said, his arm brushing mine. "This place gives me the creeps."

The alley made a sharp turn up ahead, and I hurried to the bottom, only to be greeted by the tinkling of a dozen different chimes. The chimes were made from all sorts of unusual materials, like spoons, fishing lures, and, in the case of my favorite, plastic dinosaurs with tiny bells dangling from their feet. Mountain Musings sat nestled in a cozy nook with a lime-green door—usually propped open—and cheery murals of flowers and unicorns outside to brighten up the otherwise dreary brick.

Except today the door was closed.

"Okay, I'm sensing a freak-out coming on," I said, even though I don't like to think of myself as freaking out, but let's be serious, my gift-buying plans had "impending doom" written all over them.

"Look, there's a note," Calvin said. He read the piece of sketch paper taped to the front door. "'Mountain Musings is closed so that we can attend our annual meditation/yoga retreat. Best of luck, fellow artists, and see you back next week.'"

"Next week?" I said. My mouth had gone numb like I'd just left the dentist. "But it can't be closed. I preordered my gift days ago! It's a mug with Vincent van Gogh's face, and when you add hot liquid, he loses an ear. It's perfect!" I rattled the knob—it was locked—and banged on the door, and then waited, before banging some more.

This. Could. Not. Be. Happening. Mountain Musings was the only place to get art stuff in all of Tanglewood Crossing, unless you counted the Walmart one town over, but they only had crayons and markers and little-kid paints, and Mom was a real artist.

"There's always Wal—"

"Don't even!" I said, and then I felt bad because maybe I sounded a little mean, but I could tell that Calvin understood, because . . . Calvin.

I banged some more, and Calvin helped, before I finally gave up and sank into a lump on the concrete. "That's it. My plan is officially ruined."

Calvin slid down beside me. "What is that thing your mom always says? That if we just walk and let the world speak to us, we'll get inspiration. We could try that."

"How can I walk around when I'm busy crawling into a cave to starve to death?"

"Hmm, true. But you'll have to get to the cave somehow, right? Unless you learned how to Apparate without telling me." I looked at Calvin, because once again, rude, but did I mention that he has this way of smiling that always makes me feel better? As in no matter what, which is great, but also weirdly annoying.

I glared. He smiled. I felt better. What is up with that anyway?

"Fine, let's walk. But this is so not good. My plan had five parts. Five very important parts, and if I leave one out it's . . ." I racked my brain for the right word. "I don't even know! It's not a plan!"

"Come on, we'll figure it out." He helped me to my feet, and we started up the dreary alley.

You know in olden times when people would walk behind dead bodies and there would be all this crying and sad music, because they were going to somebody's funeral? That's what it felt like. Also, it was really steep, and even though I live in the mountains, my thighs aren't made for climbing.

Still, I tried to stay positive. I wasn't just a matchmaker. I was a problem solver. When one door closed, another one opened, right? Sure, sometimes you had to force it open, with a crowbar or dynamite or something, but so what?

This was happening.

We could do it.

Cre-e-e-e-a-k!

We were halfway up the dark and creepy alley when it happened. A door, a literal door—remember the one from before that was painted in shocking pink—eased open, hinges shrieking. I might, occasionally, be dramatic, but Calvin literally jumped, screaming, and then tripped on a cobble and fell, dragging me down with him.

"Dramatic much?" I said, dusting myself off and helping Calvin to his feet. I held my breath, checking the poster board that was lovingly stuffed in the side pocket of my backpack. The Sign of Perfect Beauty and Sparkliness was, thankfully, undamaged.

"Sorry." Red splotches crept up Calvin's cheeks and neck. "Can we pretend that never happened? As in erase it from your memory forever?" He stared down at his shoes, mortified, and I decided to go easy. Calvin could be a total wimp some-times, but he was still my best friend.

"Pretend what never happened?"

"You know, the whole me falling on my butt thing . . . oh . . . right. Thanks."

"No worries. Hey, let's go inside."

"Wait, what?!"

"Look, there's a sign." It was true. I had totally missed it at first, but now that I looked closer, I saw a single line of printed text, no wider than a pencil, taped to the outside of the door.

"'The Shop of Last Resort: Purveyor of Mysteries,'" I said, reading the sign aloud. "This could be just the place to find a unique and totally non-Walmart-related gift. You were right, Cal! All we had to do was walk around a little and, whammo, inspiration!" I swung the door wider, but Calvin lingered on the steps. "What? You're not still scared, are you?"

Calvin tore his eyes away from his shoes and met mine. If I was reading his eye feelings right, he was totally freaked, but doing his best to be brave. "Me? Scared? Not in a zillion years. Come on."

CHAPTER 2

THE SHOP

We stepped inside. The Shop of Last Resort was . . . not even being dramatic here . . . amazing! And not at all what I'd expected. What had seemed kind of creepy from the outside—what with all the long, drawn-out creaky noises—turned out to be anything but.

This place looked like a magic shop and a fantasy unicorn tea party had gotten into a fight, and they'd both won. The walls were covered in pink velvet wallpaper that sparkled in the light from a dozen tinkling chandeliers. I drew in a sharp breath as a toy train, decked out in purple sequins, chugged past my head, horn blasting. It was riding on a track suspended in a tangled spiral from the ceiling. I watched for a moment as it climbed ever higher, weaving in and out of the gently swaying chandeliers. Every once in a while, it sent up puffs of purple smoke that filled the air with smell of grapes.

All around, customers milled about, oohing and aahing at the strange objects packed onto the hodgepodge of shelves. Most of the customers, tourists from the looks of them, sipped from steaming cups of tea and giggled as they read aloud the pink tags dangling from the objects.

"'Laugh-o-Matic Specs,'" said a lady in a bigfoot T-shirt, holding up a pair of giant star-shaped sunglasses with a cracked lens. "'Never look at the world the same way again.'"

She poked her friend, a lady with hair like a baby-blue beehive, and shoved the glasses over her friend's ears. Her friend gasped, and stumbled. The plastic lenses swirled like oil slicks, in alternating shades of pink and purple. And then beehive lady started to laugh. Really laugh. As in bent-over, tummy-rattling laughter.

"What's wrong with her?" Calvin said, squeezing in close to my side to let more customers pass.

"No idea," I said, but I watched in wonder as a group of customers huddled around beehive lady, each begging for a turn with the apparently amazing specs. "What is this place?"

"It must be new," Calvin said. I followed his gaze as he struggled to take in all the weird stuff smushed into the small, cramped space. The whole shop was about the size of my trailer, except rounder and packed with shelves.

It was hard to get a good look at it all, with so many people squished together, but we couldn't miss the huge unicorn, like from a carousel, with only half a horn. The tag read, "Dr. Sparkles, MD, heals minor cuts and bruises."

"Yeah, right," Calvin said. "This place is so weird."

Weird, and awesome. I stared into the unicorn's bright blue eyes and couldn't help but shiver with excitement. It was all so cool and strange and totally unexpected. I was sure to find the perfect gift!

I slid my hand into my pocket and my heart sank. In all the panic and excitement, I had forgotten that I only had two dollars to my name. I'd used the rest of my money to buy Mom's other gift, the one currently locked inside Mountain Musings. And I couldn't ask to borrow money from Calvin, because I knew he was saving up his allowance to buy a new mod for his favorite video game, *Monster Deli.*

Tragedy.

Clouds of doom and gloom.

"Look at this," Calvin said. It was clear from his eye feelings that the excitement was starting to rub off. He pointed to a stoplight with two missing bulbs and read the tag aloud. "'The All-Seeing Traffic Signal. Lights up green whenever you're thinking about cake.' Did I mention this place is super weird?" Calvin said, scrunching up his forehead.

I nodded, trying to force a smile, but I could feel the rain cloud growing bigger over my shoulder. Soon, I'd be drenched in my own personal rainstorm of failure.

I let Calvin drag me around the shop, showing me item after amazing item. Like a chipped teapot that claimed to make any kind of tea taste like Earl Grey, a broken alarm clock that would chime any time your dog needed to poop, and a half-melted microwave that could turn any liquid into pea soup. Supposedly. But it was hard to focus on all that when I could see my Welcome Home, Mom plans falling apart. Literally. In my brain, the list I'd made to ensure maximum party awesomeness caught fire and crumbled into a million charred bits.

Party over.

Future ruined.

How could I forget my tragic lack of funds? Two dollars! That wasn't enough to buy anything good, even at the Megastore-That-Shall-Not-Be-Named, aka Walmart.

"Hey, are you okay? You look kind of like you're freaking out." Calvin had stopped in a nook filled with broken toys. He looked at me with his deep brown eyes, and I had to admit, I felt a little less freaked.

I took the two dollars from my pocket and showed him the crumpled bills. "Two dollars, huh?" he said, rubbing his chin. "Cool. That should be plenty."

"What?" I said, wondering if I'd stepped into some bizarro universe in which Calvin suddenly forgot how money worked. "Two dollars. As in less than three. As in not enough to buy anything good ever, and can I crawl into a cave and starve now?"

Calvin's face split into a grin. "Um, no. Definitely not. Haven't you been looking at the price tags? Everything in here is super cheap. Like creepy cheap. That unicorn thing back there cost five bucks."

"What?" I grabbed the nearest thing I could find, a Barbie with a missing head that claimed to give you perfect curls if you slept with it under your pillow. "Twenty-five cents? What is this place?"

"That's what I said." Calvin laughed. "Come on, let's find something for your mom. It's getting late."

Yikes.

Double yikes!

"Did you see the time?" I said, in a totally nondramatic manner. "We only have five minutes before Dad comes to pick us up!"

That got me moving. We squeezed past tourists in bigfoot T-shirts and those foam foot hats, looking for anything Mom might like. Her main interests were painting, Vincent van Gogh especially; New York, her hometown; and sketching, which is basically painting, except with pencils or charcoal.

We nudged our way into every nook. "Is it weird that all this stuff is broken?" Calvin asked, staring up at a shelf of broken kitchen supplies. "And what's with the tags? Are we supposed to believe this stuff is actually magical?"

"I don't think so," I said, hurrying down the only aisle we had yet to explore. "I think it's supposed to be a joke. Like, 'Hey, look at this broken thing, isn't it totally useless? But wait, it has a funny label, let's buy it.'"

"Marketing strategy," Calvin said, rubbing his chin again. "Smart. Ooh, I bet we can find something in there."

The last aisle was mostly filled with stuffed animals, all covered in stains with the stuffing spilling out. They smelled too, like dusty barf, but at the end was this giant wooden crate packed full of junk. On the side of the crate, someone had written in glittery black paint, "Odds & Ends: Everything $1."

"One dollar?" I liked the sound of that.

I dove in—not literally dove, but you get the idea—wading through broken Game Boys, Frisbees, a waffle maker with only the top half, pink skates with no wheels, a deflated bike tire, a bent retainer. "It's useless," I said, giving the crate a kick. That sent the junk inside tumbling, to reveal an object of true and utter perfection. A ball of tingly awesomeness swelled inside my chest as I pulled the piece of torn canvas free. It wasn't just any ordinary piece of canvas. The cloth looked old and yellowed on the back, and on the front was . . . a painting.

An impossible painting.

An amazing, perfect painting that Mom would totally love!

I ran a shaky finger over the uneven ridges of paint. The image itself wasn't that great, two boring sunflowers, one faceup, the other facedown. Also, it had a big tear down the middle, like the artist had gotten angry and decided to destroy his own work. The cool thing, the totally perfect thing, was that I recognized it. Remember how I said that Mom was obsessed with Vincent van Gogh? He's probably most famous for painting *The Starry Night*, but he also did this whole series where he painted nothing but sunflowers.

These were sunflowers.

Torn-up, kind-of-ugly sunflowers, but still.

Obviously, it had to be a copy. I'm not totally and completely naive, but it was still really cool. Epic, actually, because Mom collected knockoffs of great paintings that she found at garage sales. She liked to hang them in her art studio/ closet, because she said the copies reminded her that even ordinary people should try their best to be great. This painting would fit in perfectly with her collection.

I traced the brushstrokes all the way to the bottom left corner, and there, in faded yellow paint, was a signature: *Vincent*. "Vincent" was underlined, just like in the other copies Mom had in her closet. Some of them she'd even done herself, like the one of *The Starry Night*.

"Come on," I said, grabbing Calvin by the sleeve and hurrying to the front. The cash register was painted sparkly silver, and it sat on a table covered in thick white fur. "Who do I pay?" I said, somewhat frantic, dinging a bell that was poking out of the fur. "Hello? I'm ready to check out."

A beaded curtain behind the counter jingled. I looked up. The sign above the curtain read RESTRICTED SECTION: NO ENTRY. Ooh, can you say mysterious? Any other time, I would have investigated, but Dad was almost here.

I gasped as a woman emerged from behind the curtain. This time, I was the one who grabbed Calvin's hand. She wasn't scary, exactly. She wore a hot-pink feather dress, lace-up army boots, and a silk scarf twisted around wild white hair. Her milky eyes twinkled, capturing the light from the chandeliers, and she tilted her head at me, amused.

But she was old. Don't get me wrong, I think old people are totally amazing, like Gram, but this lady would have looked right at home in a sarcophagus from ancient Egypt. Her skin dripped down her face in long, crinkly folds that jiggled as she approached the counter. Her earlobes drooped down almost to her shoulders, and I could trace each of the thick green veins snaking beneath her papery skin.

"Um . . . aren't we in a hurry?" Calvin said, giving my hand a squeeze.

That jolted me right out of my stare-fest. I let go, cheeks burning, as I realized what the old lady must think of me.

"Sorry, I didn't mean to stare. I just need this." I held up the painting and slid a dollar across the fuzzy counter. That was when a lump of wrinkles the size of a soccer ball appeared at her side, hopping up next to the register, rolls wiggling.

"Whoa!" Calvin squeaked, but the old lady didn't seem to notice him.

"Well now, I see we have a savvy young lady in our midst," she cooed in a sweet, syrupy voice that matched her clothes, but not so much her age. "Aren't you precious? And you have quite an eye. Not many young people care about art these days."

"It's for my mom," I said, but I wasn't paying much attention thanks to the wrinkle ball that turned out to be a cat. It was shaped, literally, like a soccer ball, with two bulging yellow eyes, a saggy mouth, and a few patches of striped fur. Where the fur had fallen out, its skin looked like one of those super-wrinkly dogs, if you left it in the bath for a few hours and then wrung it out to dry. Oh, and its skin had stripes too, kind of like a shrunken baby tiger.

"I see you've met Mr. Winkles. Isn't he the sweetest?" she said, nuzzling his ancient forehead. "All right, hon, I guess that'll do it. Come see us again sometime." She dug a business card from under the counter and held it out to me. I took it gingerly, careful not to touch her fingers or any of Mr. Winkles's jiggly folds. Not that I'm against wrinkles, or cats. Like I said, I adore Gram, but these two . . . I don't know. They gave me the creeps. "'Ms. Imogene Magpie: Purveyor of Mysteries,'" she read aloud. "But you can call me Mag." She winked, and then rolled up the painting and stuck it in a purple bag speckled with stars. "Don't be a stranger, you hear? Come back soon!"

She waved, even though I was standing right there, and smiled so big I could see the edges of her false teeth. "Thanks," I said, a tiny shudder running up my spine. Mr. Winkles turned, flashing his bony tail and bare bottom. Gross.

"Wait," Calvin said, turning back once we were almost out the door. I could tell he was ready to leave, but his voice sounded curious. "That painting . . . it doesn't have a tag."

Mag's smile widened. "That's because you got it from the Odds and Ends bin. Isn't it exciting? There's no telling what it might do!"

With that, Mag moved on to help other customers, leaving Calvin and me to share our own private freak-out moment. I checked my watch.

Triple yikes!

"Let's run!"

A moment later, we were zooming up the alley, racing through the shadows and back into the sunlight, the old lady and her cat forgotten. At least for the moment. Dad was probably already waiting for us outside The Friendly Bean. True, it wasn't like Dad would leave us behind, but if we didn't leave now, we might be late picking up Mom at the airport. That was so not happening. Especially now that I had the perfect gift.

"Faster!" I shouted as we weaved around the Bigfoot Burritos food cart. Calvin may have long legs, but I'm way faster, despite my refusal to enjoy anything involving running. I slowed down a little as we neared Sasquatch Sweeties, because Calvin was wheezing—a lot. Also his face was turning red, and he had sweat dripping into his eyes, which is maybe why he didn't see the tour bus whip around the corner at that exact moment.

The big yellow bus with the giant hairy foot on top came barreling around the bend just as Calvin was crossing the street. I grabbed his shirt and pulled him back, screaming something heroic like, "Watch out!" Spoiler alert: He did not get squashed to death by a bigfoot bus. Phew. But he did fall on his butt and splat into a huge mud puddle. This was so not a happy day for Calvin's butt.

"Holy bigfoot, are you okay?" I said, bending down to help him up. That was when I saw the sign. Our sign. The most glorious, resplendent WELCOME HOME sign the world had ever seen, melting into a swirling puddle of rainbow mush. I checked in the purple bag to make sure the painting had escaped unscathed. It was fine, but the sign . . . Step three of my perfect plan . . . ruined.

An engine roared behind me, and I knew it was Dad pulling up to the curb in his old-as-the-hills pickup. I didn't turn around. The sight of that sign melting in the puddle was just too darn tragic. I couldn't look away. In fact, I sank down right next to Calvin, not even noticing the water seeping into my favorite jeans.

"Hey, honey pie, you okay?" I still didn't turn around, but there was Dad lifting me out of the puddle like I didn't weigh any more than a soggy flour sack. He put one strong arm around me, the one covered wrist to elbow in tattoos—my favorite was this one of an angry mermaid riding a motorcycle made of fire. He smelled like cigarettes and motor oil and peppermint mouthwash, which might not sound like that great of a smell, but it really was. "You two get in a fight with a mud puddle?"

Maybe I should explain a little about Dad. He's what

you would get if you took the leader of some biker gang, taught him a bunch of country slang, mixed in about a million tattoos, and then, just for fun, decided to make him basically the kindest, sweetest person you could ever meet. Seriously, he bawled at the ends of *Charlotte's Web* and *The Giving Tree*, which are both super sad, so understandable, but once he even teared up at a dog food commercial. Not even kidding.

"It was my fault," Calvin said, peering down mournfully at my sign. Not gonna lie, his sad face made me feel a little better, because I could tell he really cared. But still, tragedy had struck. And right when I thought everything would turn out perfect. "I'm the worst at running, and now I ruined everything. Kill me. Go ahead, put me out of my misery."

"That does sound bad," Dad said, handing me and Calvin each a spare bandana so we could wipe off. "Is that your sign for Mom?" Dad said, poking his boot at the soupy, rainbow-colored puddle that had once been a true masterpiece. Dad knew all about my list—I was a big fan of lists—since I'd spent the past two weeks going over each and every detail.

"Not anymore, thanks to me." Calvin's shoulders slumped and his eyes got this embarrassing watery stuff at the edges. If you ever doubted that Calvin had real superpowers, don't bother, because I couldn't stay mad at that kid for one more second, not with such a heartfelt declaration of guilt.

"It's okay. I've still got Mom's gift." I gave Calvin's shoulder a punch, which was my way of saying we were a-okay, even though my plan was kind of falling apart. *Think positive*, I told myself. I showed Dad the painting. It seemed to shimmer in the sunlight, and for the first time I found myself wondering if it really did have some hidden magical properties.

"Is that for Mom? Dang," he said, holding out the word nice and long. I could tell he was really impressed because he even whistled, which is one of his special talents, along with flipping a quarter between his fingers, stuffing not one but two entire hot dogs in his mouth, and the main one, being able to fix just about anything. "An authentic Vincent van Gogh knockoff, huh? Hey, you might be a secret treasure hunter, baby."

He examined the back of the canvas, checking out all the puckers and age spots. "Heck, your mama's gonna lose her cornflakes when she sees this." That was one of his country sayings. He says he learned them from his gran, who passed away before I was born, but just between you and me, I think he makes them up. "Hey, who knows, maybe it's not a knockoff. We should take it to that *Antiques Roadshow*. Make us a hot million."

"Dad," I groaned, tapping my watch.

"Nah, hear me out. We'll get you on that TV, make you famous, then I'll retire and you can support your old man. What do ya say?"

I knew he was totally making fun of me, but not in a mean way. Also, Dad couldn't retire, since he didn't exactly have a job. He just fixed stuff around town whenever it happened to break.

"Focus, please. We're going to be late." My plan was already melting into rainbow goo at my feet. The last thing I needed was to miss Mom getting off the plane.

"All right, you're no fun today. Calvin, my man, you riding with us?"

Calvin looked over at me with, I'm not joking, eyes like the world's saddest puppy. "If it's okay with you. I did ruin everything."

"Come on, get in." I gave him another punch, harder this time, and we climbed into Dad's truck, leaving the former best sign ever to its watery grave.

CHAPTER 3

WELCOME HOME

If you grew up in a big city, or even a medium- sized one, then you probably have the wrong idea about the Tanglewood Crossing airport. It's basically one gray building with a landing strip and a guy named Merle to greet you when you go inside. Baggage claim is what they call the curb out front where another guy, Eddie, will drop off your bags after hauling them from the plane in his pickup.

Dad popped in to say hello to Merle, while Calvin and I claimed a prime spot on the curb. Seating was limited, and this elderly couple with a just-okay WELCOME HOME sign had already snagged the only bench. You might be wondering why a small town like Tanglewood Crossing even needs an airport, but then you would be underestimating the popularity of our most famous resident, bigfoot. Oh, and I forgot to mention that there's a bigfoot statue right outside the front doors.

As it got closer to time for the day's one and only flight to arrive, I could feel my own personal rain cloud looming over my shoulder. I told myself I was being silly. Just because the sign got ruined, it didn't mean my life was about to explode. I would finally get to hug Mom for the first time in five weeks, so what was I so afraid of? It wasn't like the world would suddenly stop because I'd failed to mark one little thing off my list.

Probably, everything would be fine. We'd have a party, with cake and presents. Everyone would sing happy birthday to me—because, oh yeah, turning twelve here—and then Mom would tell me all about her awesome time at camp.

I ordered myself to chill and took a few calming, non-dramatic breaths. The curbside filled up with excited friends and family, chattering happily and carrying balloons or flowers or more just-okay signs. We should have picked flowers. Why hadn't I thought of that? All I had was a painting of ugly sunflowers and a nonexistent sign.

Dad came back just before seven, when the flight was set to arrive, and we all looked up at the sound of a whirring engine. Right on cue, the clouds parted and the white belly of the plane came into view. I don't know what it's like where you're from, but in Tanglewood Crossing everyone stands and applauds when the tires touch down, even the tour bus driver in his yellow uniform waiting to take tourists to our one and only hotel.

At the sight of that plane zooming down the runway, I realized just how silly I'd been. Mom was back. The birthday/welcome home party would be totally awesome, just like the picture on my vision board. Me and Mom and Dad back together again, the way it should be.

Once the applause died down, we all waited for Eddie to drive over in the stair car so the passengers could disembark. By the time the doors opened, my whole body was vibrating with excitement. Dad stretched out tall, peering over the heads of the people in the crowd, and we both watched, waiting to see Mom's frizz of pink hair—according to her last letter, that was her new color—and her chunky sunglasses and her holey jeans, which she always wore on long trips, because she said they were easier to lounge in.

The first person off was a guy in all camo with a matching backpack, and the old couple from the bench rushed over to hug him. I saw Dad tear up a little watching those three, but he tried to hide it under his long biker-guy hair. A bunch of other people got off too, but not Mom. I remember thinking how I couldn't wait any longer, because I'd already waited five weeks and enough was enough already. Then this guy in a blue uniform came out, and he looked kind of like the pilot, and then the plane door closed.

My heart dropped down into my stomach, but I told myself not to panic. She was probably just gathering up her stuff, since Mom always packed a million things anytime we went on a trip. I waited some more, watching that door for the slightest hint of movement. Any second now, it would open and everything would be okay.

The door stayed shut. All around us people were laughing and heading to their trucks.

Calvin looked at me, and I looked up at Dad. He had that little frown he gets sometimes right between his eyes, which meant this was bad. As in really bad. I could see Dad trying to work out what to do, and I could feel my heart squeezing with panic.

"I'm sure she'll be here any second," Calvin said, nudging my shoulder, but I didn't answer.

Then I heard this ringing sound that I hadn't noticed before with all the happy-people noises, and it was someone calling Dad's cell.

He whipped out his ancient flip phone and checked the caller ID. I couldn't see what it said, but the frown between his eyes got deeper. He took a few steps away and said, "Hey, are you okay? Where you at?"

His voice sounded kind of growly and mean, but that's the secret thing about Dad: His voice always sounds kind of growly and mean, but it never actually is. Dad was quiet for a long time, which meant the person on the other end must have been talking. I tried to look at Dad's face, to read the feelings in his eyes, but his shaggy hair was blocking my view, and besides, he turned away.

Maybe it didn't really happen, or maybe it did, but I swear the air got heavy and silent, and everybody else in the world disappeared. Time stretched out, and the air kept on getting heavier and heavier and pressing in on my throat, and then Dad said, "Don't do this. You promised we'd tell her together . . . [pause] . . . No, I can't, because we're already at the airport because you said . . . [pause] . . . No,

listen . . . [pause] . . . June planned a party. We can't just . . ."
Dad walked off, hair still covering his face, and I could tell
he wanted to be alone. I followed. "We can't do the party
tomorrow like we talked about, because it's happening
tonight, on her birthday. People are probably headed to our
house right now . . . [pause] . . . What? Do you want me to
just leave them out there waiting? . . . [pause] . . . I didn't
tell you because it was supposed to be a surprise."

I watched Dad deflate a little more with each word, and
the air got so heavy I was sure I would suffocate and sink
down into the pavement and never get up again, but I didn't.
"Fine, have it your way, then. I guess I'll see you tomorrow."

Dad snapped his phone shut, and even though I couldn't
see his eyes, I could tell how he was feeling, because I was
feeling that way too. Also, he did this thing where he moved
his jaw back and forth, kind of like a cow chewing cud, and
that meant he was trying to figure out how to tell me something he didn't really want to tell me. Like that time when I
was little, and I screamed at him to watch out, because there
was a turtle in the road. And we stopped, and he got out to
check, and then he had to tell me that the turtle was squished
and living in turtle heaven.

"She's not coming, is she?" I said after a while, because

Dad never did come up with any words. Despite all my positive thinking, the worst had happened. I'd tried to make everything turn out perfect and this was what I got.

He took a few deep breaths and wiped the hair out of his eyes. "She'll be here tomorrow," he said. "She decided to drive back instead of fly." I could tell that wasn't the whole story, but I could also tell that every word hurt on the way out, like he was coughing up stones instead of telling me a simple fact. He kept working his jaw and chewing his lips, and that's also a thing he does when he's trying really hard not to cry.

Like I said, my dad cries a lot, but he's not a wimp. He just can't help it. He looked so sad in that moment, I wanted to reach out and hug him, like that day with the dog food commercial, but something held me back.

"What did you mean?" I said, that heavy air tightening around my throat. "What were you and Mom going to tell me together?"

Dad looked away, and then I could feel Calvin standing beside me. That helped a little but not a lot, and then Dad put his arm around me and we walked side by side back to the truck.

I didn't know then what was about to happen, but I knew

it was something big. I could feel it, like the heavy air and the strange silence and the tightness in my throat that didn't go away even when we started driving.

I took out that ugly painting right around the time we passed the gas station. The sun cast these long, creepy shadows down the petals. I remember watching how the light shifted and changed as we drove along the empty highway, and I remember how, with each mile, the petals seemed to wither and dry out, dying slowly the closer we got to home.

When Dad pulled up to the trailer with the clinking spoon wind chimes and beer bottle sculptures in the front yard, the air was just as still and rotten as if I really was carrying a canvas full of dead flowers.

I climbed out and held the painting up to the sun to get a closer look. I expected it to be a trick of the light, but it wasn't. The vibrant yellow-orange petals had turned to twisted brown husks. I tilted the canvas, watching as one of the stems appeared to shrivel, oozing yellow puss. It had to be an optical illusion, like one of those holographic images that changed depending on how you looked at it. Any other day, I might have thought it was cool, but what good was a painting that withered and died the more you looked at it?

Some gift.

Dad climbed out of the truck, telling Calvin to go inside, and he said four little words that made me forget all about that creepy painting.

"Hey, honey pie. We need to talk."

CHAPTER 4

THE TALK

There was no party. No Mom. No look of surprise when I gave her the now-super-creepy dead flower painting. Just me and Dad sitting under the carport on two milk crates, one scooted up against the other. After, when it was over, I remember being glad we were sitting side by side instead of face-to-face, because then I didn't have to look him in the eyes when he told me.

He scooched right up close and wrapped his arm around me, and he kind of pulled me into his sweaty armpit. I couldn't see his face—like I said, that was a bonus—but I could tell from his voice that it was one big ache. "You know how much we love you, right, baby? Me and your mom?"

I tensed up big-time, like a mouse when it spots a cat, because I already knew where this was heading. Except it couldn't be. It was like I'd woken up in *The Twilight Zone*— which is this old show Dad and I totally love—and some creepy nurse peeled the bandages off my eyes, and suddenly I realized that everything I thought I knew about the world had been a lie.

I didn't answer. What I really wanted to say was, "Shut up. Shut up already!" Because I knew that if Dad kept talking, he would say something I didn't want to hear. Something impossible. So I just sat there, a ventriloquist's dummy with a wooden mouth and brain, and Dad kept right on talking.

"This art camp your mom's been at . . ." He paused, chewed his lips. "It wasn't just about the art. Your mom and I . . . [longer pause] . . . we've been talking things over for a while now." He looked down, his greasy hair brushing my face. I wanted to collapse into his chest and never get up again, but I sat, wooden, alone, Dad's voice drifting farther and farther away.

"We both decided it'd be a good idea to try some time apart." His head dropped lower, like it was suddenly too heavy for his shoulders. "What I'm trying to say is . . ."

Don't, don't, don't! I screamed the word inside my head. Dad couldn't hear me. Why couldn't he hear me? I was screaming so loud, over and over, but my mouth stayed shut.

"Your mom and I are getting a divorce."

What I remember most is not moving. Like I said, I'd basically turned to wood. Wood was better, because those wooden ventriloquist dolls didn't have any feelings. Dad wrapped his other arm around me too, and he said, "I'm so sorry, baby, but everything's going to be fine. Promise."

And I remember screaming at him in my head and calling him a liar, because how could everything be fine? Yeah, it didn't help. I was a wooden girl with wooden eyes full of wooden feelings. At least that's what I wanted to be. Instead of shouting or moving, I sat there, breathing in the reassuring smell of his sweaty T-shirt, and then we heard tires crunch up the drive, and Dad said, "Shoot, don't move. I'll be right back." He squeezed me one more time, his face in that big, scrunchy ache, and jogged over to head off the person in the big red truck.

It was Carl, Mom's boss from the gas station, and I could hear Dad explaining how I was sick and so we'd have to postpone. Carl drove away, but then more cars pulled up, and Dad had to keep stopping them before they could get out and explain how we'd had to cancel the party. I sat there. Alone with my thoughts. Alone is not a place you want to be when you wake up one day and find yourself trapped in *The Twilight Zone.*

The crate next to me creaked. Calvin came over and sat down beside me.

"Hey," he said.

I didn't say anything. Wooden girl, remember? Also, I was pretty sure I'd forgotten how to breathe.

"So, I kind of heard everything."

More silence. Me wondering how long I could live without taking a breath.

"That stinks about the party." The muggy heat settled down all around us. A june bug buzzed over from the grass and settled on my leg. I stared at it. I couldn't even lift my hand to swat it away. Calvin reached over and gave it a flick. "Not just about the party. I mean . . . you know, the other thing."

"Yeah, I know." My voice sounded like tires on gravel, or maybe that was the people driving away, but at least it was back. Sore, but still working.

We sat there and watched the june bugs dancing in the grass, and I tried not to stare directly at the sun as it dipped below the scraggly trees.

When all the cars were finally gone, Dad came back. He looked down, hair in his face. He scratched the back of his neck. "Crummy party, huh?"

He offered to drive Calvin home, but we ended up eating the pizza that Dad had forgotten to cancel and watching like five episodes of *The Twilight Zone* because at least it was better than talking.

After that, I rode with Dad when he drove Calvin home. Calvin gave me this look before he got out, and not kidding, I could see everything he was feeling in his eyes: that he was sorry, and that life stinks, and that he wished he knew exactly the right thing to say to make it all better. Looking back, I don't think there was a right thing.

I climbed into the front seat, and Dad took off down the winding, empty highway. Usually, driving at night with Dad, just the two of us, was one of my favorite things in the world. The headlights glowing against the cool asphalt, Tanglewood Forest stretching out all dark and mysterious on either side of us, Dad singing off-key to heavy metal, and me with my head hanging out the window, letting the wind eat up all my laughter. And I definitely would be laughing, because Dad might be a lot of things, but he sure as heck wasn't a singer. Usually, I would be happy, but I had a feeling that *usually* didn't matter much anymore.

"Hey," Dad said. His voice was rough gravel, all sad and sore just like mine.

"Hey."

"You wanna talk about it? When everybody showed up, and then Calvin, I . . . I should try to explain."

"No." I didn't mean it to come out so sudden, but I wanted Dad to stop talking. I wanted it all to stop and go back to the way it had been. And it would. Even if I had to make a million more plans and execute them each perfectly. In the morning. When my head didn't ache. "Not tonight."

He drove on for a while, hands gripping and ungripping the steering wheel. "Mom should be in town tomorrow. She said we can still have a party. If you want. And she's sorry for missing your birthday."

He looked over at me, and I didn't even have to answer. That guy could read me like a book. "All right, no party. I got your presents though and—" He stopped. I knew what was about to happen, because I could feel it tight in my throat, like Dad and I had this weird connection and I knew what he was going to do before he even did it. He got real quiet, and his achy face scrunched up worse than before, and he let his hair fall in his eyes and cranked the radio up full blast the rest of the way home.

Later, Dad brought me my presents when I was getting into bed. He sat down, and the mattress sank under his weight. I wished I was a little kid again so he could crawl in next to me and read a story.

"You wanna open these now? It's still your birthday."

I shook my head. Dad's face was hidden under all his hair, but I could tell his cheeks were still red from the car. "All right, in the morning, then." He squeezed my knee and sat there awhile longer before getting up and turning off the light. "Love you, baby," he said, silhouetted there all wild and shaggy in the doorway.

"Love you, Daddy."

He clicked the door shut, and it was just me alone with the shadows. I lay still, sweat trickling down my back, thoughts thudding like june bugs inside my skull. The rain cloud that had been trailing me ever since Mountain Musings turned hot and heavy, wrapping around my throat.

I wished I had my own phone, so I could text Calvin, but Dad couldn't afford one. So I was stuck with my thoughts. And my thoughts kept drifting back to last year's vision board. It looked a lot like this year's, a poster filled with drawings and photos and magazine clippings. My main goal had been to convince Mr. French, the drama teacher, to put on *Bigfoot in Paris: A Love Story* as that year's school play. It's basically the best play ever, and not just because Gram wrote it.

It took a lot of planning and lists and hard work, but finally I convinced Mr. French to put on the play. I'm a problem solver, remember? Except, not so much. The play turned out to be a total disaster. At first. The gazebo where bigfoot proposes to the mermaid collapsed during the second act. Bigfoot spilled tomato soup all over his costume, the Eiffel Tower melted under the hot lights, and Mr. French's cell phone rang during the big dance number. Total. Disaster.

Then I'd had an idea. That's the power of positive thinking for you. I rushed around backstage, whispering instructions to all the actors. In the final act, we made even more mistakes, but this time they were on purpose. The mermaid tripped on her tail fin and ended up facedown in her own wedding cake. Bigfoot's mother wore a rubber chicken on her head in place of a hat, and the villainous hunter, who came to capture bigfoot before he could tie the knot, slipped on a banana peel and split his pants.

It worked. When we stepped onstage for the curtain call,

the audience roared with applause. Because of my quick thinking, they all thought the play was *supposed* to be a comedy, instead of a huge mistake.

That meant the divorce would work out too. As in not happen. As in I would be the one to stop it.

All I needed was a plan. I know, I know, my first plan had failed. Majorly. But it's not like that was my fault. A soggy sign wasn't responsible for Mom missing my birthday, or the Divorce—notice that capital *D* as in oh-so-dire. I knew that now. This was bigger than any sign. Bigger than anything I'd faced before.

But I could do it. When things fall apart, I find a way to fix them. Presto change-o, positive thinking magic. Oh, and I'm a matchmaker now too! If I can't convince Mom and Dad to stay together, who can?

Yes! I would fix this. Absolutely!

In the morning.

When my brain wasn't a heaping bowl of mush.

CHAPTER 5

HELLO, FUTURE ME

I pushed off the covers and slid onto the carpet, where it was cooler. My brain needed some major chill time. I lay down in the square of light coming in from my one big window, staring up at the ceiling fan and my bigfoot mural and the dirty beige blinds. Dad always kept the floodlight on out front, and it brought the moths and crane flies and other flying bugs with their big veiny wings. It was kind of gross, but also kind of nice, the way you could hear the gentle brush of their wings against the glass. Maybe I did have a little artist in me after all.

I lay there awhile, trying not to think, but the thoughts

kept right on bobbing up to the surface. Tired and upset and willing to do anything for a distraction, I decided to go ahead and check out my presents. I didn't plan to open any.

You can probably guess what happened next.

I picked up a square box wrapped in newspaper with a huge duct tape bow. Dad could do just about anything with duct tape. That bow was a beautiful sight to behold. I only meant to loosen up the tape a little to get a peek inside, but the next thing I knew I had unwrapped the most epic bigfoot alarm clock in history. It had this huge plastic bigfoot with a clock in its belly, and the sticker on the bottom said, WAKE UP TO THE GROWLS OF THE MYSTERIOUS WILD MAN. I could tell it wasn't brand-new, because bigfoot had a few scratches on his cheek, but the clock was ticking away just like it should be, and that was good enough for me.

The next present was a pair of bigfoot socks complete with hairy toes and, inside, about a pound of chocolate. Awesome.

The last present was a total mystery. I told myself not to open it, but, yeah, you know how that goes. I picked up the long, flat rectangle, weighing it in my hands. It was super heavy. I had no idea what could be inside. What better way to find out than to lift off the lid? Dad had left a sticky note, written in his big, scratchy script: "Didn't get a chance to fix the screen yet, but it works. Hope you can use it."

I peeled back the newspaper to reveal a laptop. It was totally ancient, and huge, and the screen was split with one big spidery crack, but that laptop was the most gorgeous thing I'd seen in years.

Maybe I should stop to explain. I'd never had my own computer, let alone a laptop or a cell phone. Even Mom and Dad still used old-timey flip phones that couldn't do anything but call or text. We weren't exactly rich, but we had everything we needed, like our trailer, and Dad's truck, and plenty of food to eat, just none of that other fancy stuff.

But this . . . I pressed the button in the corner and waited for my new baby to power up.

It took a while, but boy was she beautiful. And that's not all. Dad had put a bunch of pictures on the desktop. Of me and him and Gram in our hiking gear back when I was nine, posing next to this mammoth footprint. It turned out to be a bear footprint, according to Gram, but it was still pretty cool. There was one of Mom painting my face at Halloween. That year, Dad and I had gone as tinfoil aliens, like from our favorite episode of *The Twilight Zone*, and Calvin had made a spaceship costume out of cardboard and duct tape.

I looked through the rest of the pictures, and that was when I noticed a tiny black label just below the screen. The silver letters said REFURBISHED COURTESY OF THE SHOP OF LAST RESORT. I flipped the laptop over, looking for a pink tag like on the other items in the shop, but didn't find one. Maybe Dad had taken it off, or maybe he'd found it in the Odds & Ends bin like with my painting. What a strange place to buy a laptop. How had Dad even found the place?

My new discovery got me thinking. I found the purple bag where I'd tossed it on the floor and unrolled the painting. Even in the dim light from the screen, I could see that some of the petals had perked back up. Half were still brown and brittle, but a few had turned yellow again, arcing up toward an invisible sun.

Weird. I held the painting at different angles, to see if it would change depending on the light, but the picture stayed the same. Double weird.

I browsed around on the laptop some more, checking the settings and turning on the Wi-Fi. I knew how laptops worked, obviously, since I'd spent so much time using Calvin's. I connected to the free trailer park Wi-Fi and held my breath. I'd been waiting for this moment my whole life.

My very own computer. No more begging Calvin any time I needed to type something for school because our ancient desktop had decided to stop working again. It took a lot of spinning and refreshing, but I finally got a web page to load: Dr. Eliza Day's bigfoot blog, of course. I surfed around awhile, relishing the awesomeness of the moment, before deciding to message Calvin.

I knew he liked this messaging app called Hi-hi!, so I downloaded it, which took just under one million years, and then I sent him a contact request. He didn't respond. To be fair, it was 2:27 a.m. according to my brand-new(ish) bigfoot clock. Yikes!

I wondered where Mom was at this hour, and if she was awake. I wondered why she hadn't come home. Didn't she love Dad anymore? Had she totally forgotten about my birthday? Was she planning to move back to New York, and if so, would I ever see her again?

A message popped up in Hi-hi!, along with a quiet ping. Finally, distraction.

I expected it to be from Calvin, because who else? But the username said JUNIEPIE28. Dad called me Junie Pie sometimes, though not so much lately. I blinked at the words on the screen.

JUNIEPIE28: Sorry, kid, but you can't change her mind. It's not about you.

I watched the little cursor blinking on the screen, waiting for me to type in my response. My fingers hovered over the keys. Outside, the moths kept up their nighttime dance. I wasn't going to type anything because gross, creepy stranger, but my curiosity got the better of me.

BIGFOOT_GRL: Who r u?

I watched those three scrolling dots appear below my message, so I knew the creepy stranger must be typing.

JUNIEPIE28: I'm you. From the future.

Okay. Not weird at all. What kind of internet troll would pretend to be me? That's just . . . gross.

BIGFOOT_GRL: No, for real. Who r u?

Scrolling dots again. Maybe it was because it was the middle of the night and I never stayed up this late, but my

Freak-o-Meter was suddenly wide-awake and whirring. It had to be some troll playing a joke, right? Maybe Calvin trying to be funny, except . . . he still hadn't accepted my contact request, so I was pretty sure he couldn't message me. *Ping!*

JUNIEPIE28: Clean the spiders out of your ears, kid. I'm you. I just said. You didn't think this was a normal laptop, did you?

Major. Freak-out. Time. "Clean the spiders out of your ears" was one of Dad's down-home sayings, and like I said, I'm pretty sure he makes them up, so . . . who the heck was I chatting with?

JUNIEPIE28: Sigh. If you want to get technical, I'm an alternate version of Future You existing in a parallel timeline, but forget about science. This is magic, remember? The important thing is, I'm here to help.
JUNIEPIE28: Hello? Paging Alternate Me.
JUNIEPIE28: Don't freak, okay? I remember all about freak-out mode, trust me, but try to chill for once. I'm on your side.

BIGFOOT_GRL: Calvin? This is so seriously not funny!

JUNIEPIE28: And I'm so seriously not Calvin. How else can I say it? I'm. You. As in you from an alternate universe created specifically to facilitate this magical interaction.

I thought back to all the pink tags claiming that the objects in question had magical powers. But that had been a joke. A marketing gimmick to get tourists to buy a bunch of broken junk, right? Yes, obviously. Magic wasn't real. It was made-up, like leprechauns or gnomes or monkey hands that grant wishes. Of course, a lot of people thought bigfoot was made-up too. No! I was being ridiculous. It wasn't the same at all. Was it?

What had Mag said about the items in the Odds & Ends bin? Not that they weren't magic, just that they were unpredictable. No. Come on, brain, don't even go there. This had to be some kind of trick.

JUNIEPIE28: Look, you don't have to believe me if you don't want to. Like I care. You're probably thinking that magic isn't real and this must be some kind of trick, yeah? Whatever. Pretend I'm a stranger if that helps. Just a wise old soul reaching out through the internet to give you some helpful advice.

It ended up that even my Freak-o-Meter had a breaking point, and JUNIEPIE28 had just pushed me way past the red line. So far past I almost wanted to laugh, because there was no way this could be happening. It was silly, impossible . . .

JUNIEPIE28: Oh, by the way, remember how you always wanted to get a flaming mermaid tattoo, just like Dad's? Well, you did it. Wanna know where?

No. Freaking. Way. No one knew that I wanted to get that exact tattoo, not even Calvin. Not even Dad. My fingers tingled as they hovered over the keys, trying to decide what to type next.

BIGFOOT_GRL: So this is actually a magic laptop?
JUNIEPIE28: I knew you'd catch up eventually. But don't get too excited. Magic is way overrated. Actually, that's kind of why I'm here.

BIGFOOT_GRL: Ooookay.

My brain was still locked in this-is-all-a-trick mode. But . . .

BIGFOOT_GRL: So where did you get the tattoo anyway?

JUNIEPIE28: Yeah, sorry, kid. No spoilers. What's the fun in that?

BIGFOOT_GRL: What? You just said . . .

JUNIEPIE28: Oh, what the heck? I guess spilling the beans about a little tattoo won't bend the fabric of reality or anything. Let's hope.

BIGFOOT_GRL: Bend the fabric of what now?

JUNIEPIE28: Right ankle, next to that big bumpy foot bone. And, yes, it totally hurt.

I sat back, blinking at the screen. This couldn't be happening. True, the shop had been weird, unbelievable even, but this was . . . I didn't have any words.

But if it was real, then maybe I could ask about—

JUNIEPIE28: Anyway, let's get down to business, okay? Some of us actually have lives. Whatever you're planning to do to fix the whole divorce thing, don't. Got it? D-O-N-T, don't!

BIGFOOT_GRL: Hang on, that's why you're here?

JUNIEPIE28: Look, I know it's the last thing you want to hear. It feels like the end of the world, right? Like you stepped into an episode of *The Twilight Zone*, and you'll never get out again. But you so totally will.

Remember how I said my brain was mush? In that moment, it was like someone had taken that mush, boiled it, zapped it in the microwave, and left it to be devoured by wild dogs.

JUNIEPIE28: Not that you'll feel better right away. It'll take time. Things will be weird at first, different. Point is, everything that's about to happen, you can get through it.

Three dots appeared below the last line, scrolling. I waited to see what she would type next, but then the dots vanished. The part of my brain that had turned to mush was so freaked, I wanted to close the laptop and never open it again. But the other part . . .

BIGFOOT_GRL: How do you know I'll get through it? Mom and Dad are . . . Mom and Dad. If they're not together, that changes everything. All of my plans, my life, everything.

I would have written more, but my hands and my fingers and pretty much my whole body had started tingling. It was like that feeling you get standing on the end of a diving board, waiting to jump off, only stronger.

JUNIEPIE28: Because I did.

JUNIEPIE28: And it wasn't because I made the perfect list, or followed the perfect plan. And those vision boards I used to make, OMG! Like gluing down a bunch of pictures could change the future.

BIGFOOT_GRL: Hey!

JUNIEPIE28: Sorry, just saying. Forget about perfect. Oh, and forget about that magic stuff too. Don't even go there!

BIGFOOT_GRL: Wait, what? Aren't you talking to me on a magic laptop right now?

JUNIEPIE28: Yeah, but that's different. Look, pretend I didn't say anything. Besides, my memory's kind of fuzzy on the whole M-word front. That whole wild summer, one big blur. But I remember enough, and I'm telling you, don't mess with it. No matter how bad it gets. Divorce sucks, sure, but it's not the end of the world. Magic just might be.

BIGFOOT_GRL: Not the end of the world!

JUNIEPIE28: That's what I said. Man, you are such a drama queen!

BIGFOOT_GRL: Rude! You do realize that you're insulting yourself?

BIGFOOT_GRL: And what are you saying anyway? That I should just give up? Let Mom and Dad get divorced, even though they so totally love each other? It's my life too. Or maybe they forgot about that part.

JUNIEPIE28: Look, kid, it's complicated. And it's not about you. Getting Mr. French to do that bigfoot play was one thing. Planning and positive thinking, am I right? I remember how much you love that stuff. This is other people's lives we're talking about. Trust me, it's different.

BIGFOOT_GRL: Mom and Dad are not other people. They're . . . my people . . . our people.

JUNIEPIE28: Sigh. Self-involved much? Look, I've gotta split. Class. But do me a favor. Try to chill out, for once. You'll thank me later.

With that, the little green dot next to JUNIEPIE28's icon turned gray. I hadn't noticed before, but her icon was a cartoon microscope. Did that mean she was some kind of scientist, or maybe studying science? I clicked on her profile. Most of the fields were empty. No information apart from her username and a date of birth: July 9, 2008. Same as mine.

I shut the computer with a satisfying click and sank back on the carpet. As soon as I did, my certainty about JUNIEPIE28 started to fade. True, she had known a lot about me. Impossible stuff, but maybe I *had* told someone about the tattoo. Yikes, or maybe someone had read my diaries. Calvin knew all about the divorce, Mr. French, almost all of it. But no way it could be him. He'd never do that to me. Why would he? It was all so totally . . . confusing. I closed my eyes, listening to the moth wings fluttering against the glass. JUNIEPIE28 was a fake. She had to be, but I couldn't help but wonder . . . what if? What if?

CHAPTER 6

DAZED AND CONFUSED

When I woke up, all sweaty and groggy on the carpet, my first thought was, *Hey, I'm twelve.* I looked over at my vision board, at all the happy pictures and glitter. Then I remembered about The Talk. In my brain, the vision board shattered, like it was made of glass instead of paper, the angry shards showering down on the carpet.

Now I would never get what I wanted, like Mom coming home, or finding bigfoot, or finishing Honey Pie, i.e., the motorcycle Dad and I have spent practically my whole life repairing. Calvin thinks vision boards are silly, because how can gluing a bunch of pictures on a poster board change the future? I used to think he was so wrong. It's called the power of positive thinking, hello! But maybe he's been right all along.

I sat up and opened the laptop. A vague memory of chatting with someone pretending to be me floated to the surface of my mind. It was like that feeling you get when you know you had a strange dream, but no matter how hard you try, you can't remember the details. I was certain it had happened. I had chatted with some so-called Future Me, who had blabbed on about magic and alternate timelines. But surely . . .

I opened Hi-hi!, searching for a log of last night's chat. I found the friend request I'd sent to Calvin—he still hadn't answered—but nothing else. Weird. Maybe Hi-hi! didn't save old chats.

Oh well. I had enough problems without worrying about some possibly made-up troll from another universe. I heard Dad rummaging around in the kitchen and made an unsuccessful attempt to rewrap my presents. Yeah, he was so gonna find out.

A few minutes later, I sat down in the kitchen nook, and Dad served up three huge plates of bacon and eggs.

"Morning, hon. You sleep all right?" He patted the seat next to him, which had this little rubber cushion so you didn't hurt your butt on the hard wooden bench. I sat down, the air whooshing out of the rubber pad. I kept my eyes on the third plate. Dad must have seen me looking, because he said, "Mom said she'd stop by. So we could talk."

The spinning that had settled down in my head from the night before started up again full blast. Mom was coming. Today, right now, and we were going to *talk*. Except I didn't want to talk, not like that, not again. Talking meant bad news, and what I wanted was for everything to go back to normal. I hadn't even had time to come up with a new plan.

"How you feeling?" Dad pressed his palm to my forehead and rested it there a minute. "You're a little hot. Hang on, I'm gonna take your temp."

"No, Dad. I'm fine."

"You sure?" He had that little frown between his eyes again, but he sank back down into his own rubber cushion.

"Yeah, I'm sure." Except, I wasn't.

"All right, then. You hungry? I made some eggs."

"I can see that." By "some eggs" he meant three heaping plates with even more eggs left in the pan.

He let out a long sigh, his body melting back into the bench. Our dining table was in this kind of cubby, so we could lean right back against the wall when we wanted. "Life stinks sometimes, huh?"

"Pretty much." I touched Dad's mermaid tattoo, and he put his hand over mine. The tattoo. That reminded me of something from last night's chat. I scratched the inside of my ankle, wondering.

"I wish things could be different, but Mom'll be here later. She can help explain."

I didn't know what to say to that, so I didn't say anything. Dad gave my hand a squeeze and then took a bite of eggs. "Better eat up while they're still hot. Mom might be a while."

I watched Dad eat. It used to embarrass me the way he eats, because only half the food ever makes it into his mouth, but then I figured that was just Dad being Dad. Also, it's pretty funny.

Mom still wasn't there by the time Dad stopped eating, leaving half his eggs and all his bacon. "We can open your presents now if you want. Or we can wait for Mom, up to you."

I guess the guilt was pretty obvious on my face, because Dad laughed out loud. He has this great laugh where his face gets scrunchy and his shoulders shake and he makes the whole table wiggle. "You take after your old man, you know that? I never could wait for nothing. Not that we ever had any presents when I was growing up, but there was this one Easter." His laugh grew deeper, the shakes spreading to his arms. "They had one of them egg hunts at church, and I snuck out early. For real, it was still dark, and there was me sneaking around town all of six years old." He laughed into his hand, remembering. "I stole each and every one of them eggs, and when we showed up later for the real hunt, all you could hear was the sound of kids crying. Sorry, I shouldn't laugh." But he did, and I did too. "Never would have found me out neither, but I ate so much candy I barfed all over the dinner table. Mom marched me right up to the church next day and made me confess."

"You never told me that," I said, snorting with laughter, happy for the distraction.

"Yeah, I was a little hell-raiser back then."

"And now?"

"Now?" Dad got up, pretending to be offended, and then mussed up my hair, which was annoying, but not really in a bad way. "Now I'm a freaking angel, what are you talking about? I gotta pee."

"Dad?"

"Yeah?"

"Thanks for the presents. They're perfect." A memory

drifted back up to the surface. I really needed to get more sleep. The label! The laptop had been from The Shop of Last Resort too, just like the painting. How could I have forgotten?

"Cool. Oh hey, did you see my note? I'm gonna fix that screen soon as I get the money. Did you test it out? It work okay?"

"It works great." Thoughts swirled in my head, and I tried my best to piece them together. "Dad? That laptop. Did it come with a pink tag?"

"Oh, you been to that shop, huh? Read all them funny tags? Gotta admit, it's a good way to get people to buy a whole bunch of junk. But nah, I got the laptop from this dollar bin and then fixed her up. You get on the Wi-Fi okay?"

"Yeah, no problem."

"Nice. Hey, if your mom comes, tell her I'll be right back."

Mom didn't come.

Not that morning and not that afternoon. Dad kept trying to cheer me up by telling cheesy jokes and squirting soda out of his nose—the usual stuff—but it wasn't working. We went out to work on Honey Pie for a while, which was usually my favorite thing, but even that couldn't cheer me up.

I was lying flat on my back, scraping rust off her recycled muffler, when I decided I'd had enough. I let my hand drop back to my side, and I stared up at the carport, at all the spiderwebs and trapped leaves. A breeze blew in, and it almost felt cool against my sweaty body.

Time to figure this out. "Dad?"

"Yeah, baby?" He wiped the hair out of his eyes, leaving a big grease stain across his face. Any other time I would have laughed.

"Do you still love Mom?"

Dad sat up, chewing his lip. The sun shone down, and his eyes were two dark slits with these big hollows underneath, because that's just how they were, hard to read and kind of mean-looking, but really kind.

"Yeah, I still love her. 'Course I do. Nothing's gonna change that."

"Then why are you getting divorced?" I'd had no intention of saying those words out loud, or what came next, but it just happened. "Is it because of me?" The words just spilled out, even though I hadn't been thinking anything like that before. Or maybe I had. Maybe I'd been wondering ever since the airport—no, ever since Mom left—if the real reason she'd gone was because of me. Something I'd done wrong. A checkbox I'd failed to tick. Something, anything, that would explain why my life was suddenly falling apart.

"No, Junie. How could it be because of you? You're—" It shouldn't come as a surprise that he couldn't finish. Like I said, Dad gets real emotional sometimes, and he can't help it. That's just Dad being Dad. He pulled me into a hug, even though we were both sweaty and stinky, and his body kind of heaved in these big, shaky sobs, and a few seconds later it was over. He sat back and wiped his eyes, but his face was still all red and scrunchy—the bad kind of scrunchy. He took some long breaths, and then he said, "You're the best thing that ever happened to me. To both of us."

He had that achy look on his face, but at least he didn't cry anymore, which was good because whenever he cried, it made my whole body hurt.

"Why, then? Why did you all of a sudden decide to get divorced? I don't get it."

"Baby, it's complicated." He went back to chewing his lip and taking these long, soothing deep breaths.

"Is it Mom? Did she stop loving you?" I didn't want to say those words either, because I knew they would sting— and how could anyone stop loving Dad?—but I had to know.

He didn't answer. He just kept on chewing at this piece

of skin on his bottom lip, and then his phone rang and he got up to answer it.

A minute or two later, he came back over and knelt down beside me. "That was Merle. Says the stair car broke down over at the airport. Needs someone to fix it before tonight's flight." I could tell he didn't want to go, but maybe he didn't want to stay either, because then he'd have to give me an answer. "You'll be all right for a few hours by yourself?"

I thought about saying no, but it's really hard to say no to Dad, especially when his face is all raw and red from crying. "Sure, I'll be fine."

"All right. Call me if you need me."

"Okay."

He squatted there awhile longer, then gave my shoulder a squeeze and headed out. I wasn't mad at Dad. I wasn't even mad at Mom. I just needed answers. Someone couldn't just come along one day, out of nowhere, and tell me that my whole life was about to change. Right? There should be rules against that sort of thing. Mom and Dad should have at least asked me before making any big decisions.

I had to figure out why they wanted a divorce. That was step one. Then, once I knew why, I could find a way to fix it.

I dialed Mom's number on the house phone and waited. Even though I needed to hear her voice, the other part of me was dreading the moment she would pick up.

She didn't. Pick up.

"Hey, Mom. It's me . . . [pause] . . . I'm just wondering where you are . . . I . . . I guess I need to talk. Call me back soon. Oka—?" The phone beeped, cutting me off.

I went back to my room. Because it was so hot, I pulled up my shirt and lay down right on the air vent. The laptop was sitting a few feet away, where I'd left it. I ran a finger over the black sticker, then lifted the screen. It woke up even slower this time, or maybe I just had a harder time waiting.

Hi-hi! opened automatically with a whoosh, and I saw that I had two new messages. My heart seized in my chest. Was it the mystery chatter from last night? Memories rolled in like waves, washing over my brain. She'd said she was me, from the future. It had all seemed so real, and she'd known details, impossible details. I scrolled down, heart pounding, but it wasn't my mystery guest.

CALTHEDESTROYER: Hi.
CALTHEDESTROYER: Are you okay?

The messages had come through a few hours ago, but I saw the green light still blinking next to Calvin's icon, which was a ghost sandwich from his favorite video game, *Monster Deli*.

BIGFOOT_GRL: Not so much.

Calvin started typing right away. I could see the little dots scrolling at the bottom of the screen.

CALTHEDESTROYER: Are you still having a party?

BIGFOOT_GRL: Doubt it. Mom never showed.

CALTHEDESTROYER: Did you talk to your dad?

BIGFOOT_GRL: Sort of. I don't know.

BIGFOOT_GRL: I think maybe Mom doesn't love him anymore.

CALTHEDESTROYER: How do you know?

I was thinking of how to answer when I heard a ping and looked up to see a new message box pop up on the screen. Whoa, this was it! All the weirdness of the night before flooded back. JUNIEPIE28, the mermaid tattoo, her warning me not to do anything about the divorce. As if. And she'd been rude! The way she'd treated me like a baby with no life. Is that really the way I turn out?

JUNIEPIE15: Hey, silly pants. What are you even talking about? Of course Mom loves Dad.

If bigfoot had burst into my room right then wearing a tiara and leather pants, I don't think I could have been more freaked. Who in the heck was JUNIEPIE15? I clicked back over to my conversation with Calvin.

BIGFOOT_GRL: Hey, did you just message me from another account?

Dots scrolling.

CALTHEDESTROYER: No, why? What happened?

A new message popped up in the other chat box. I wanted to ignore it, but how could I? As if one alternate me wasn't enough.

JUNIEPIE15: It's me, not him. Duh. I'm you when you were seven.

BIGFOOT_GRL: Seriously?

JUNIEPIE15: Hello, can you even read? I'm the one who's in second grade here. I'm you, from 2015. That's why I have that 15 at the end of my name.

BIGFOOT_GRL: Oookay.

This was so not happening. Again. I took some deep, calming breaths, like Mom had taught me, but it totally wasn't working. I thought back to when I was seven, learning to type on our ancient desktop. If this was real, wouldn't I remember chatting with my future self back in second grade? Or maybe not, if JUNIEPIE28 had been telling the truth about alternate timelines.

JUNIEPIE15: Fine, don't believe me. See if I care.

I stared at the screen some more, wondering if I should just close the chat box. Past Me was starting to give me the creeps. But still . . .

JUNIEPIE15: At least I'm not the one asking silly questions.

BIGFOOT_GRL: Hey, no need to be rude. And what do you mean, silly questions? Like what?

JUNIEPIE15: Like does Mom still love Dad? Duh, she totally does! They kiss like ALL THE TIME! Even when I'm trying to watch *SpongeBob,* and it is so, so GROSS!

Part of me wanted to laugh, because I remembered what it was like. Trapped on the couch in between them, and how grossed out I used to get, and how Dad would keep right on kissing Mom, even though I was screaming and gagging, and then he'd lean down and blow a bunch of raspberries in my ear. The other part of me was beyond freaked.

Ping.

CALTHEDESTROYER: Are you still there?

BIGFOOT_GRL: Yeah, sorry. Got distracted.

I thought about spilling the beans about JUNIEPIE15, but what could I say? Dad accidentally bought me a haunted laptop. "Haunted" wasn't even the right word. What did you call it when your past and future selves started talking to you via IM? Bad news bears, that's what you called it. I decided to keep my impending mental breakdown to myself for the moment.

CALTHEDESTROYER: You really think your mom doesn't love your dad?

Good question. My fingers hovered over the keyboard. *Ping.*

JUNIEPIE15: Hello, why don't you answer him?
BIGFOOT_GRL: Maybe I don't know what to say.
JUNIEPIE15: Duh, yes you do!
BIGFOOT_GRL: No, I don't, and stop being such a know-it-all. It's complicated.

Wow, seven-year-old me was super annoying too. What was that about?

JUNIEPIE15: Is not.
BIGFOOT_GRL: Is so.

JUNIEPIE15: Not! Anyway, why don't you just ask Mom if you don't believe me?

Now, that stopped me in my tracks. But I'd tried. Mom wouldn't answer her phone.

Ping.

CALTHEDESTROYER: June?

BIGFOOT_GRL: Sorry. I don't know if she still loves him, but I need to find out.

I thought about calling Mom again, but I'd already left a message.

Ping.

A third chat window popped up. Great. What now?

JUNIEPIE28: Not to butt in here, but I might be able to help.

JUNIEPIE28: Are you there?

JUNIEPIE28: A simple hello would be nice.

Freak-o-Meter to the max. Actually, I'm pretty sure it was broken by that point. I was already chatting with my seven-year-old self. Why should the sudden reappearance of Future Me come as a surprise?

JUNIEPIE28: Remember me? From last night?

JUNIEPIE28: Fine, ghost me if you want. You try to reach out and help a fellow you, and this is the thanks you get. I'm logging off.

BIGFOOT_GRL: Wait!

JUNIEPIE28: Not exactly the warmest welcome, but it'll do.

BIGFOOT_GRL: You're Future Me, right? From 2028?

JUNIEPIE28: Now you're catching on. Maybe you're not such a total diaper baby after all.

BIGFOOT_GRL: So how many others are there? Alternate versions of me, I mean?

JUNIEPIE28: Who knows? You didn't grow up and become a secret genius. I'm just you. Well, better, obviously, and with boobs, but basically the same.

BIGFOOT_GRL: I've got boobs!

JUNIEPIE28: Yeah, no you don't. Anyway, I've got like actual stuff to do, so let's make this quick. If I remember right, when Mom first came back she was staying near Dino Land. Man, that place is sad. But yeah, you'll find her by that pond she likes in a silver RV. It's totally huge. You can't miss it.

BIGFOOT_GRL: Hey, Dino Land isn't sad!

JUNIEPIE28: And I'm not telling you this so you can make some grand Let's-Fix-Everything plan. Got it? I'm telling you this so you can talk. You and Mom.

JUNIEPIE28: And Dino Land is SO sad. Trust me, I am your elder.

BIGFOOT_GRL: Stop talking to me like I'm a baby!

JUNIEPIE28: Rude much? This conversation is officially over.

BIGFOOT_GRL: Wait, don't go! I have questions.

Phew, she didn't log off. At least for the moment. This whole chat might be impossible, as in so totally, but I couldn't deny it any longer. This was happening. Like Gram, aka Dr. Eliza Day, always said, "If you find enough evidence for something, even an impossible something, then it must be true." And, hey, maybe Future Me really could help.

BIGFOOT_GRL: Why doesn't Mom just come home so we can talk? Why stay away?

BIGFOOT_GRL: Was it something I did?

JUNIEPIE28: Sorry, kid, I'm not Google. You can't ask a question and expect me to give you all the answers.

JUNIEPIE28: But no, it's not your fault. Like I said, this whole divorce thing is so not about you.

BIGFOOT_GRL: What, then? Is it Mom?

BIGFOOT_GRL: Did she stop loving Dad?

JUNIEPIE28: Go talk to her. That's what you, I mean *I*, should have done in the first place. Stop trying to fix everything for one second and just talk. Promise?

Future Me was turning out to be a real pain.

JUNIEPIE28: Hello, are you still there?

BIGFOOT_GRL: I'm here. I just . . . What should I say when I see her?

I watched the dots scroll at the bottom of the screen.

JUNIEPIE28: You'll figure it out. Just do me a favor and don't be too hard on her. It's complicated, you know what I mean?

I didn't know what she meant, even though I'd just said

the same thing to seven-year-old me. The green dot next to JUNIEPIE28 turned gray. I clicked back to JUNIEPIE15, but she had gone too. Great. So much for helping me in my time of need. And why did JUNIEPIE28 keep telling me to stop planning stuff? Had Future Me totally given up on life or something?

I did some actual deep breathing to calm my nerves, then clicked back to the conversations I'd just had with the JUNIEs. Once again, all evidence of our chats had disappeared. Weird. And now that the chat boxes had closed, the details of our conversations were already getting fuzzy in my brain. Double weird.

Whatever, the important thing was I knew what I had to do. The divorce wasn't my fault, and it wasn't because Dad had stopped loving Mom. That only left one possibility. I had to take JUNIEPIE28's advice.

BIGFOOT_GRL: Cal?

CALTHEDESTROYER: June?

BIGFOOT_GRL: Are you up for a top secret mission?

CALTHEDESTROYER: Do you even know me at all?
Two questions: When? And where?

BIGFOOT_GRL: Dino Land. Ten minutes.

June's Extra-Thick Planning Notebook, p. 325
Talking to Mom Checklist

- Bring the sunflower painting (check) (All the petals are yellow now BTW! So weird!)

- Pack the strawberry Twizzlers in case a celebration is in order (check)

- Ask the Big Question, i.e., does she still love Dad? (future check)

- Take a bunch of deep, calming breaths on the way. This is so not a good time for a freak-out. (definite future check)

CHAPTER 7

THE STRANGER

Once I had all my plan gear packed, along with the usual stuff—pocketknife, flashlight, magnifying glass, evidence collection bags, because you never know when you might encounter bigfoot—it was go time.

I paused in the doorway, wondering if I should call Dad. The phone was sitting right there on the wall by my head. I laid my hand on the cool green plastic, but decided to leave a note instead. Notes were good. Great, in fact. No way Dad could tell me to wait until later to talk to Mom if I left a note. Did I mention how not-good I am at waiting?

"Riding bikes with Calvin. Be back soon," I scribbled,

and then I stuck the note on the six-pack in the fridge, so he'd be sure to see it. Not that Dad cared about me going out. He was super chill about me riding bikes and going into town and stuff by myself. That might seem weird to fancy, big-city folks, but in Tanglewood Crossing, it's totally normal. It was the Mom part I was worried about.

I pulled out onto the highway—riding on the shoulder, of course—and pumped my legs as hard as they would go. Gravel sprayed out from under the front tire, pricking my bare legs. My muscles burned, my lungs squeezed, the sunlight bit down on the back of my neck like a shark spitting fire. But I didn't mind. In fact, I liked it. I was moving, things were happening. That meant I was one step closer to achieving my goal, i.e., fixing this whole divorce thing. I could have kept on riding all night, tearing up that road, but then I saw the crumbling sign for Dino Land, with the cheesy-looking brontosaurus and the faded-out T. rex, and I jerked the handlebars, sending the bike into a skid.

The world spun by, the ground hurtling up to meet my head.

"Are you dead?" Calvin asked a minute later. I looked up to see him hovering over me, blocking out the sun. A wave of relief washed through me. Not because of the bike or the fall or my ugly scraped elbows, but because Calvin was Calvin. Normal. Something I could count on.

"Nope, just slowly bleeding to death." That skid had been . . . kind of epic, and not in a wow-isn't-this-awesome kind of way. To be fair, I was totally fine, but still a little shaky.

"Oh. That's good." He helped me to my feet, offering a crooked smile. As always, he kept a tiny pack of wet wipes in his back pocket—his mom is a total neat freak—and he handed me a few to clean up.

"So, what are we doing at Dino Land?" he said, peering warily at the six-foot fence and the curls of rusty razor wire. "Didn't you almost get shot here once?"

"Technically, yes."

Maybe I should explain a little about Dino Land. According to Dad, it used to be this really awesome theme park. People would come from all over the world to walk with the dinosaurs. Full disclosure, the dinosaurs don't actually walk, or look real, but they are life-sized, and for kids back then I guess that was pretty cool. Anyway, now it's not so much an awesome theme park as a dinosaur graveyard.

Don't get me wrong, I still totally love it. It's closed off to the public now, but Dad and I sneak in at least twice a year to take pictures next to all the old dinosaurs. One time, the owner, this guy named Daryl Hicks, came running at us with a shotgun, shouting for us to leave, but Dad being Dad, told him off. Next thing I knew, that guy Daryl was inviting us in for tea.

"But we're on a secret mission, so danger kind of comes with the territory," I said, giving Calvin a punch for courage. I hid my bloody wet wipes under a rock, and we headed off on foot, me in the lead and Calvin trailing a few feet behind. As we made our way through the woods, I could see his eyes drifting off into the park, taking in the crumbling plaster dinosaurs, the broken carousel with its raptors instead of horses, the weeds, the blowing trash, and the puddles of sewage that had been left to stew and fester.

"Are we about to get murdered?" Calvin said. He came up beside me, and his hand brushed mine. I was pretty sure it was a mistake, but not totally. I slid my hand into my pocket.

"Let's hope not. Anyway, we don't even have to go inside. The place we're headed is just outside the fence."

"That's a relief," Calvin said, wiping fake sweat from his brow.

We ducked under vines and avoided puddles. Calvin got

"attacked" by a spiderweb, his words. He's so not a fan. Then we came to the edge of the fence, turned right, and there it was: the pond.

Mom's pond. A small pool of deep green water buzzing with mosquitoes and dragonflies, sunlight reflecting off the glassy surface, a weeping willow at the far end, branches drooping down to kiss the water. Her secret spot. Where she went to paint, and think, and get away from me and Dad.

Except now it was different, because this huge silver RV blocked my view. It looked like a submarine on stilts, and there was this shiny red car, the kind city people drove, parked at the head of the submarine.

"I think I hear someone," Calvin said, but I put a finger to my lips and motioned for him to stay back.

The trees rustled at the far side of the pond. For a strange moment, I thought I saw a pair of wild yellow eyes watching me from the shadows, nonhuman eyes, but then something moved inside the RV. I froze, my gaze darting to the silver door. I waited for someone to appear.

This was it. My moment to ask Mom the big question. Did she still love Dad? No, wait. I should give her the painting first, soften her up a little.

I watched, muscles growing tenser by the second. I

waited for the submarine door to open and for Mom to step out. Nothing happened.

After a few minutes, I returned my gaze to the trees on the far side of the pond, but the mysterious eyes had vanished.

I crept forward. Deep. Calming. Breaths.

I should just go knock. What was I waiting for? Then I finally heard a door open, followed by footsteps squishing over the wet grass, and I plastered myself against the side of the submarine. From where I was standing, I could see Mom, but she couldn't see me. She padded over the grass in bare feet and took a seat on a wooden stool, facing a mostly blank canvas. The pink had faded from her hair, except for the tips, and those looked like melted cotton candy.

I watched as she dabbed her brush in some paint, held it up to the canvas, then let her hand fall back by her side. She kept taking these short, shaky breaths and blinking her eyes at the canvas, but never laying down any paint.

I started to walk over, to finish the rest of my plan, but something stopped me.

It was just so weird seeing her sitting there, all alone, blinking her eyes, almost like she was trying not to cry. Mom never cried, unlike Dad. And why should she? Up until yesterday, everything had been fine. At least I thought it had. What could have changed between now and then?

Mom turned her head, like maybe she could hear me breathing. She stared off into the trees, back toward where Calvin was hiding. I held my breath. I'd come here to talk, so why didn't I want Mom to see me?

Maybe part of me was afraid of what she might say.

Mom turned back around, lifting her brush to the canvas again, and I slid the painting from my bag. A few of the petals had started to wilt again. I ran my fingers over the thick brushstrokes, searching for hidden wires, some kind of screen. The gloppy ridges chipped under my nails, just like real paint.

The wind picked up, rushing through the nearby branches, and suddenly I could smell Mom like she was standing right next to me. She smelled like paint, of course, and bug spray and banana-scented sunscreen, because Mom could get a sunburn in the middle of the night on a cloudy day, at least according to Dad. She was still wearing her holey jeans, and a paint-flecked tank top and her favorite army boots, which were at least two sizes too big. Those were so Mom. She liked clothes that had character, history, not boring stuff you could buy off the rack.

I took one final deep breath. What was I so afraid of?

I stepped into the clearing.

A twig snapped under my foot, and Mom turned, surprised. It took a moment for her eyes to register who I was, like she'd been gone so long, maybe she'd forgotten. Her face fell, and she drew in a shaky breath. She stared at me for what felt like forever, and I knew I should say something, execute my plan, but my mouth had gone dry. It had been five weeks. Five weeks with nothing but a few emails and postcards. My fingers tightened on the painting without my even realizing it, and then she was up and pulling me into a hug. I hugged her back, of course I did. The past five weeks were already starting to drain away. What can I say? I didn't know then what I know now.

When Mom finally let me go, she stood back and pushed the hair out of my eyes. "He told you." It wasn't a question, but Mom searched my face for answers anyway. Her voice was breathless, worn out, exhausted. "That's good."

She sank back down onto the stool, and I watched my mom, my beautiful fairy-punk-hippie-artist mom, watch me. To be more exact, she observed me. Her eyes are this cool, pale blue color that's mostly gray. I used to lie awake at night wishing my eyes would turn that color too.

I opened my mouth, to ask the big question, but no words came out.

"You're beautiful," she said, and she was talking in her artist's voice. Her eyes were the faraway, dreamy eyes that could turn anything pretty with a few dabs of paint. "I don't tell you that enough, but you are."

"Mom, I—"

"Remember that time we drove to Louisiana when you were seven?" she said in her same dreamy voice. "The car broke down and your dad called one of his buddies to bring him a part, and so there was nothing we could do but sit on the side of the road and wait. Do you remember that?"

"Mom, I need to ask you something. About Dad. I need to know if—"

"Your dad . . ." She looked over at her blank canvas and the pond beyond, then back at me. "He said we should get out and explore, do you remember? But I was tired, in a bad mood. I lay down in the back seat, and when I found you two a few hours later, you were knee-deep in mud, hunting crawfish. The way you laughed every time he plunged his hand down in that dirty water." Her eyes drifted back to the pond, her expression so sad and beautiful and faraway. "He was telling you some story, I don't remember what, but it made you laugh. You two had your own secret language, even back then. I sat there, and I sketched you both, and I don't think you even saw me." She paused, and I could feel her tracing my features with her eyes. "I still have it somewhere. The sketch." She motioned vaguely at the RV.

"Mom," I said, louder this time. "We need to talk."

She turned to look at me, her eyes slowly coming back into focus. "Sorry. I guess I've been thinking about the past a lot lately."

We both turned as the door to the RV opened. For this weird moment, I expected to see Dad, so I couldn't understand why the guy standing there didn't look anything like him. He had on cargo shorts—Dad never wore shorts—and flip-flops, and his face was smooth, except for this ugly little goatee, but Dad always forgot to shave. My brain kept trying to turn him into Dad somehow, but he wasn't. Just some other guy, and he looked from me to Mom and said, "Oh dang, is this her?"

I flinched away from him, because I knew. In that one moment when the stranger stepped out of the trailer, I knew.

"Junie, wait. I can explain," Mom said, half standing. She didn't. Explain.

And I didn't ask the question I'd come here to ask, because what was the point?

Mom just stood there, and the guy stood there, and this totally scary anger bubbled up in my stomach. Without thinking through exactly what I was doing, I clenched my fingers down on the painting. The same ugly painting I'd been so excited to give to Mom. Part one of my second failed plan. "There!" I said, throwing it in the mud at Mom's feet. "Enjoy your gift!"

She stared down at it, and I stared down at it, and the really weird part was that the flowers had changed again. They weren't yellow anymore with hints of brittle brown, but pure black. The petals all moldy and rotten, oozing flower guts that buzzed with roaches and flies.

Even though I'd never asked, I'd gotten the answer to my question. Mom didn't love Dad. I wanted to shout some more, to hit someone, to throw another ugly painting, but instead I turned and ran.

Mom didn't follow.

Maybe I was being dramatic, but I sure as heck didn't care. I raced for the trees and smacked, hard, into Calvin. To be honest, I'd totally forgotten he was there. Our foreheads clunked together, and we fell, like something out of the world's cheesiest comic. I hit the ground, and I could feel little rocks cutting into my bare arms, but what did it matter?

What had JUNIEPIE28 said? To take it easy on Mom? Yeah, right!

I brushed the rocks off and sprang to my feet.

Calvin didn't say anything until we got back to the bikes. Which was probably a good move, because I still wanted to hit someone.

"You know," he said, careful to stay out of hitting range, "it might not be what it looks like. He might be . . ."

"What? What might he be?" I cringed at the sound of my own voice. It wasn't just angry, but hateful, so not like me, but I couldn't do anything to change it.

"We could go back and ask her. Find out for sure."

I shook my head. "No way." Calvin met my eyes, and a sliver of my burning anger drained away. Superpowers, remember? "I can't go back there."

"Okay."

We stood next to our bikes, neither of us knowing what else to say. Overhead, a wall of storm clouds pushed in. The air got that electric crackle, like it always does right before a big rain.

"We should probably head back," Calvin said.

"Yeah." A butterfly landed on my handlebars, and I slapped it away.

"She still loves him, you know." Calvin looked kind of shocked by his own words, but kept on going. "Your dad, I mean. Even if that guy is . . . the guy you think he is . . . that doesn't mean she stopped loving him. It doesn't change anything."

"What?" I could feel the anger stirring up again in my chest, even hotter than before. "How can you even say that?"

"I mean, yeah, it changes stuff, a lot of stuff, but she's still the same person she was before. Only different."

"The same person, only different? That doesn't make any sense."

"No, I'm just . . . Sorry, I'm saying it wrong. It's like, when my parents got divorced—"

"They're not."

"What?"

"They're not getting divorced." My anger was burning on full blast by now, throbbing inside my head and pushing out all my other, nonviolent thoughts. Okay, my latest plan had failed, miserably, but at least now I knew where to start. Mom didn't love Dad, at least not right now. That was information I could use.

"But you said . . . I mean, you saw . . ."

"I know what I said." I climbed on my bike, tightening

my stranglehold on the handlebars. "But it doesn't make sense. None of it does. It all started with that weird art camp. Mom went away for five weeks and she just, I don't know, forgot. All I have to do is remind her how much she loves Dad, and life will go back to normal." I could feel a renewed sense of determination building in my chest.

"June—"

"No, shut up! I don't need you to explain this to me, okay? I just want to go home."

"Okay, fine."

Calvin climbed onto his bike. He got that sad puppy look again, and I knew I sounded mean and that it wasn't Calvin's fault, but I couldn't help it. A stray raindrop hit my cheek. Great. On top of everything else, I was about to get soaked.

"Sorry," Calvin said.

"Don't say you're sorry."

"Okay, but—"

I didn't wait for Calvin to finish. I took off, pumping my legs harder than before, not even caring when the sky opened up and the rain came down in waves.

CHAPTER 8

A BETTER PLAN

Dad was outside working on Honey Pie when I got home. He sat up and wiped the sweaty hair out of his face. "Hey, hon. I was about to go looking for you. Where you been?"

I hadn't really thought about what I'd tell Dad when I got home, but I lied. Again. "Nowhere. Just riding around."

"How's Calvin?"

"You know, the same."

"All right. Come on over here and hold this muffler for me. There's something stuck up under there I can't reach."

All the bad stuff I was carrying drained away as I knelt

down beside Honey Pie and held up her rusty old muffler. It was so . . . normal. Like everything else in the world could go wrong, but this would still be the same. Just me and Dad and our broken-down, totally amazing motorcycle. I put planning mode on hold for the time being and got to work.

"Hey now, what's all that on your arm? Let me see."

I'd forgotten about the scrapes and scratches. I told Dad I fell off my bike, that it was no big deal, but he went inside anyway for the first aid kit.

That whole night, I considered telling him about the stranger. While we ate leftover pizza dipped in Tabasco sauce. While we watched *The Twilight Zone* and that show Dad loves where these guys trick out fancy motorcycles. And every hour or so when Dad went outside to leave another message for Mom. That whole time, I wanted to tell him about the other guy with his cheesy flip-flops and cargo shorts and his weird not-Dad voice, but I couldn't.

Not yet. But, one way or another, Dad was going to find out.

He fell asleep on the couch with a beer in his hand, and he looked way too sweet and serene to be disturbed. I peeled the beer from his fingers and put it safely on the table, then covered him in his favorite scratchy blanket.

After that, I decided I might as well go to bed, but it wasn't like I planned on sleeping. Not even close. It was planning time. I opened my notebook and drew a huge X through my last plan. I wrote, "A Better Plan" in thick black letters, and went into full-on Action Girl mode. I had to find a way to remind Mom how much she loved Dad. Something big. Something to make it like the last five weeks had never happened.

I tapped my pen, the kind that could write in five colors, on my notebook. I rolled onto my back and stared at the ceiling fan making lazy circles overhead, the spokes trailing these long, dusty-gray tentacles. *Think, self, think.* I wrote down a bunch of ideas, mostly terrible. I crossed them out again, wrote some more. I listened to the moths outside doing their nightly dance.

After approximately one million years of failed brainstorming, I decided to open Hi-hi! The familiar whoosh sent a prickle up my spine. I tried to start a chat with JUNIEPIE28, but, of course, she wasn't there. No previous chats. No sign of her profile when I did a search.

Great.

I messaged Calvin instead.

BIGFOOT_GRL: Hey, sorry about earlier.

The dots started scrolling right away.

CALTHEDESTROYER: No worries. I know what it's like.

Calvin's parents had gotten divorced a few years ago, back in third grade, so maybe he did know. Sort of. But this was different. This was Mom and Dad. And no way *they* were getting divorced.

CALTHEDESTROYER: Does your dad know? About him?
BIGFOOT_GRL: No.

Right? He would have said something.

CALTHEDESTROYER: Are you going to tell him?

I let my fingers glance across the keys. I was almost relieved when I heard the ping of another chat box opening.

JUNIEPIE15: Hello? Does Dad know what? It's not nice to keep secrets.

Awesome. Talking to JUNIEPIE28 was one thing. That might actually be useful. She could tell me what she'd tried, and then I could figure out how to do it better. The last thing I needed right now was to try and explain why Mom was a big fat cheater to seven-year-old me. She still thought babies came from giant clamshells that mommies and daddies found washed up on the beach. Seriously, she really believed that. I should know.

BIGFOOT_GRL: Nothing. Go away.

JUNIEPIE15: Meanie!

BIGFOOT_GRL: I said go away.

BIGFOOT_GRL: And stop snooping!

JUNIEPIE15: I'm you, remember? So stop keeping secrets, you big meanie pants!

BIGFOOT_GRL: If you're me, then I should be able to make you go away!

I shut the chat box, hoping she would take the hint. This was so not helping with my plans.

CALTHEDESTROYER: June?

BIGFOOT_GRL: I don't know if I'll tell him, okay? Not yet.

CALTHEDESTROYER: What are you waiting for?

Good question. Dad would find out sooner or later, but why couldn't it be later? He still loved Mom, he'd said so, which meant that all I had to do was remind Mom how much she loved Dad. And I could do it, I knew I could. I just needed the exact right plan. My eyes drifted up to the photos Dad had put as the desktop background. Some of my favorite moments with him and Mom and Gram. That got me thinking . . .

JUNIEPIE15: Rude!!! I was talking to you.

Double great. Had I really been this annoying when I was seven?

BIGFOOT_GRL: No, you were leaving me alone.

JUNIEPIE15: And of course Mom loves Dad, silly. I already told you. They love each other so much it's GROSS!

True. It was gross. I remembered. But something had changed in the past five weeks. *Or maybe it's been going on longer than that*, a nagging voice whispered in my head. Yikes. Am I the only one who hates naggy inner voices? Why can't they ever come up with nice things to say? Like, *Hey, self, you sure are looking great today. What's your secret?* And why do they always speak in those low, creepy whispers? Could I please have a normal, cheerful-sounding inner voice for once?

Sigh.

But inner me was right. What if something had changed between the time I was seven and now? Something I'd never bothered to notice before?

BIGFOOT_GRL: Hey, do you remember that day we broke down in Louisiana? And me and Dad went digging for crawfish?

JUNIEPIE15: Duh, that was the best day! Dad let me take off my shoes and squish my toes in the mud, and he kept pulling out these wigglers with pointy legs and beady eyes, and they were super yucky. Gag. But also amazing!

BIGFOOT_GRL: What about Mom? Where was she?

I watched for the scrolling dots, but they didn't come right away.

JUNIEPIE15: Hmm, not sure. I think she stayed in the car. Why?
BIGFOOT_GRL: Doesn't matter.

But maybe it did.

JUNIEPIE15: Is everything okay? With Mom and Dad?

I could feel my seven-year-old self entering freak-out mode. Time to put on the brakes.

BIGFOOT_GRL: Duh, why wouldn't it be? Now go to bed.

I closed the chat box again, hoping she got the message this time. But talking to seven-year-old me hadn't been a total waste. What if Mom had brought up that crawfish story for a reason? What if she felt left out? Dad and I had all the same interests, like working on Honey Pie, and fishing, and watching bigfoot documentaries on repeat. Mom liked art, and walking in the woods for inspiration, and Skyping with her New York friends who she'd met back in art school.

Was that part of why she'd stopped loving Dad? Maybe if I could remind her of all the things we did have in common, then she would change her mind about the divorce. Yes, I was onto something, I was sure of it. First with the pictures, now with the tip from my not-so-helpful self. The gears in my brain got to whirring, entering full-on action mode.

After all that time toiling and tapping my pen, the perfect plan practically hit me over the head. Blammo! Inspiration! Like one of those Whac-A-Mole games at the fair, only the mole was my brain and the mallet was the world's greatest plan.

BIGFOOT_GRL: Cal? I've got another secret mission. Are you in?

CALTHEDESTROYER: Am I! Yes! Wait . . . does it in any way involve spiderwebs?

BIGFOOT_GRL: No. Maybe. Kidding, definitely not. It involves the Bigfoot Ball!

As in the yearly dance that kicks off Bigfoot Week, a week full of nothing but bigfoot-themed celebrations. It's a Tanglewood Crossing thing. Trust me, if you lived here, you would totally get it.

CALTHEDESTROYER: Oh. Hey, I actually wanted to ask you about that. The ball, I mean.

BIGFOOT_GRL: It's the perfect plan! Mom and Dad go every year, and Dad gets all dressed up and shaves his face and everything. It's like the only time they go on an actual date.

What better time to make Mom fall in love with Dad again? Right?!

CALTHEDESTROYER: I was thinking, since we always go anyway, to help Merline and Big Vic with the food . . .

BIGFOOT_GRL: All I have to do is convince Mom to go again this year with Dad, then she'll remember how much she loves him!

CALTHEDESTROYER: Maybe we could go and, you know, not help with the food. You and me?

BIGFOOT_GRL: And then she'll forget all about weird Cargo Shorts Guy and come back home and everything will go back to normal. It's so totally perfect! Goodbye, divorce! Hello, Mom and Dad in love again!

BIGFOOT_GRL: Cal? Are you still there?

BIGFOOT_GRL: What do you think of my plan?

CALTHEDESTROYER: Yeah, sorry. Sounds great. I'm in.

BIGFOOT_GRL: Awesome. Meet me at The Friendly Bean tomorrow, 11 a.m. sharp! And bring more glitter.

TO: ladyvangogh7@gmail.com
FROM: juniepiethegreat@gmail.com
SUBJECT: Can we talk?

Mom, it's me. Sorry about today. I didn't mean to run away. Dad says you need some time to think, but can we meet? I got a new laptop, by the way, did Dad tell you?

Anyway, hope you can make it. The Friendly Bean, twelve o'clock.

See you there.

–June

CHAPTER 9

OPERATION TRUE LOVE

That night was full of some major list action, but it was all about to pay off. The Bigfoot Ball was happening in two days at the community center, which meant I had to convince Mom now that she still loved Dad. Otherwise she'd never say yes when he asked her to the dance. And a yes was so totally vital. If she said yes, that meant she still loved him and there was no way they could go ahead with the divorce.

Problem solved. No need for my whole life to go kablooey.

That was where The Friendly Bean came in. Not only

was it the best hang-out place in all of Tanglewood Crossing, but it was already super romantic on account of Merline and Big Vic being the ones who organized the ball, not to mention the Lovers' Brunch that took place every year the morning of the dance. It was such a big deal, they'd already put up most of the decorations.

"Remind me why we need so much glitter," Calvin said, sprinkling silver glitter on the red plastic tablecloth.

"Because it's romantic," I said, taping a fuzzy heart to the napkin dispenser. Romantic décor was step number one of my New-and-Improved plan.

Let me set the scene. The Friendly Bean, Saturday, eleven forty-five a.m., back booth. Like I said, the place was already pretty romantic, thanks to Merline. I'd never been a big fan of all the ooey-gooey stuff, despite my recent success as a matchmaker, but Merline was practically an expert. She gave us the tablecloth and a bunch of extra decorations. Oh, and a Heartbreaker Special on the house, i.e., one huge piece of chocolate cake with two fancy glasses of sparkling grape juice.

It was perfect.

But fancy décor was only step one. Well, technically step one had been convincing both Mom and Dad to show up here at the same time, but you get the idea. Now for the finishing touch, also known as my secret weapon. The thing that was sure to make Mom say yes whenever Dad asked her to the ball. And it had all come to me thanks to JUNIEPIE15 and Dad's desktop background.

I dug the photo albums out of my backpack, and we got to work.

Merline brought over two sodas, on the house, just as my face split into another huge yawn. Not that I was tired. More exhausted. As in I would have been a total walking-zombie person if I weren't on a mission. The whole not-sleeping thing, so not recommended.

Usually, Calvin would be chatting away any time we got together for one of my super-awesome plans, but today he stayed quiet. At the very least he'd have to tell me about the evil pastrami on rye he'd killed last night in *Monster Deli*, right? Nope. He kept his head down, a little worry wrinkle between his eyes. That was so not Calvin.

"Okay, spill it," I said. "You don't like my plan."

"No, it's . . . a plan." His scissors slipped and he accidentally sliced through my face in this old picture of me and Mom with Santa Claus. "Oops, sorry."

"No big. I've got another copy of that somewhere." I

folded my arms over my chest, giving him my fess-up-already stare. "What do you mean 'it's a plan'? It's a great plan, right? A this-will-definitely-work kind of plan?"

"Yeah, you're probably right. It's nothing."

"Really?" It so clearly wasn't nothing.

"Really."

"Fine."

Usually, I would have pressed him more, but did I mention? On a mission here. And we'd cut the time closer than I would have liked. I'd told Mom and Dad to meet me at twelve, and it was already 11:50 a.m.

Breathe, self. This was all going to work out great.

I found a photo I'd totally forgotten about, of Mom and Dad posing next to Honey Pie, when she really was nothing but a bucket of rust and twisted parts. Mom was kind of leaning into Dad, and Dad was looking down at Mom, and even though it was totally mushy-gushy, even I had to admit it was pretty cute. I taped it next to the one of Mom burying Dad in the sand at Sardis Beach and sat back to admire my work.

"Hang on, what's all this now?" Merline came over, giving my secret weapon the side-eye. "Look at you getting all sentimental with the craft supplies. And just last week you two were sitting over here, making fun of my ball."

"Us?" I said, putting on my innocent face.

"No way," Calvin added. "You're probably thinking of those other kids who always hang out here."

We both sank down a few inches in our seats, withering under Merline's deadly stare. "You know, romance isn't anything to be scared of. Miss Matchmaker over here should know all about that. Maybe you two should think about—"

"Okay, wow," Calvin interrupted. "Is that the time? We'd better hurry and finish this before her parents get here."

"All right." Merline winked. "Can't blame a girl for trying. It's hard enough for me to get this lump off his lazy butt long enough to dance." She nodded over at Big Vic behind the counter, who burst out laughing.

"Who are you calling a lazy butt?"

It was all cooing and kissy noises after that.

Yeah, even all these months later, it was still gross.

I did my best to ignore Merline and Big Vic and got back to my secret mission.

We finished the poster with all the photos of me and Mom and Dad, aka the secret weapon, and hung it on the wall at the back of the booth. That way, when Mom sat down, she'd see a heart-shaped collage featuring all her best memories with Dad. And me, in case that helped.

Five minutes to go.

Calvin and I retreated to our hiding place on the far side of the café, putting up a wall of menus so Mom and Dad wouldn't see us when they came in.

"What if they don't show up?" Calvin said, eyeing the stuffed bigfoot/cupid dangling from the table lamp. It had these huge kissy lips and a pink tutu, and Calvin gave it a funny look every time it spun around to face him.

"They will. I invited them both, and I said it was really important, so they'll definitely show."

"But you didn't tell them they were meeting each other?"

"Not . . . exactly."

Calvin's forehead got wrinkly again, but I ignored it. "How do you know he's even going to ask her?" Calvin said. "I mean, he said they're getting a divorce, right? Do you really think a few pictures will change that?"

Did I mention that Calvin can be super annoying sometimes, even though we're still best friends? "I explained this already. I know Dad said they're getting a divorce, but why? Think about it." I could feel the heat creeping into my cheeks. I'd gone through it all so many times in my head, it made me angry to have to spell it out again. "Mom goes away for five weeks, and suddenly they break up? In what world does that make any sense? Except, maybe it does."

"Ooookay. You lost me there," Calvin said, giving the bigfoot/cupid a poke so its lips were facing the other way.

"Remember that summer we went to Nature Exploration Camp? And I was all homesick at first and crying? And then do you remember how, when it was all over and Dad finally came to pick me up, I refused to leave?"

"Yeah, so what? You were like eight."

"I yelled at him and said that I hated our trailer and that Nature Camp was my new home."

"He knew you didn't mean it."

"It was like I forgot about Mom and Dad and the trailer, everything. I wanted to live in the woods forever and collect nature samples."

"But you got over it."

"Exactly."

Calvin considered. "Okay, but you were a kid, and that was a really awesome camp. This is different. Your mom is an adult."

"So what? It's the same thing. She went away for five weeks, and I bet she missed us a bunch at first, but then . . .

I don't know, she forgot. Or she met this guy and he tricked her into liking him or whatever. Look, the details don't matter. What matters is that she still loves Dad. I know she does. All I have to do is help her remember."

Calvin gave me this strange look, one I'd never seen before. His eye feelings were totally unreadable, mostly sad but also the tiniest bit upset. It only lasted a second, and then he dropped his gaze to a ding on the countertop. "I guess. I just don't want you to get your hopes up. Adults don't always make sense."

The bright lights cast long shadows down his cheeks. We'd never really talked about the day his dad left. All I remember was that I rode by one Sunday on my bike, and there was his dad, outside mowing the lawn in his khakis and his pastel-blue golf shirt, just like always. The next Sunday, he was gone.

It's not like he disappeared off the face of the earth though. Calvin still spends every birthday with him in Connecticut and most Christmases, but he doesn't like to talk about that either. "Dad" is a word you don't say in Calvin's house, not unless you enjoy super-awkward silences.

But this was different. Mom was . . . Mom.

"Heads up, kids. Operation Lunch Date is a go." It was

Merline. I'd filled her in on the details of my plan, all except for the part where Mom and Dad were getting a divorce. She thought I was setting them up for a surprise lunch date in honor of Mom coming home.

The bell over the front door dinged. I peeked over our menu wall, and then ducked before I blew my cover. It was Mom.

"Hey, there! Back at last." Merline gave Mom a one-armed hug, guiding her over to our surprise booth. "Got your table ready right over here. Oh, hang on, let me light your candles. What kind of date would it be without a little mood lighting?"

"What's happening now?" Calvin whispered.

I shushed him and slid a little farther up in my seat. Mom, mouth open in shock, was watching Merline fight with her electric lighter. She picked up one of the shiny pink cupids we'd left all over the table, examined it, then put it down again.

"I think there's been a mistake," Mom said, scratching the paint from her fingernails, which was something she always did when she got nervous.

"No mistake," Merline said, all smiles. "There we go. Finally. Vic! Put a new lighter on my list," Merline called into the back. The candles had flickered to life, casting the whole table in a romantic golden glow. "Now, you enjoy, hon. If you want anything else besides cake, just holler." She leaned in and lowered her voice. "You've got one good kid there, let me tell you. Spent all morning putting this together." She nodded over to our menu wall, and I barely had time to duck before Mom turned our way. Yikes. "I wish my kids would do something like this, but will they? Heck no! Of course, they're grown, but still, when was the last time they so much as deigned to call, let alone . . ." Merline's voice trailed off as she headed into the back. She was always doing that, talking and walking at the same time.

Did I mention, yikes? I met Calvin's eyes. We were both having a major freak-out moment. We turned in unison toward the menu wall, expecting Mom to come over and bust us any second, but then the door jingled.

Okay, this was it. It had to be Dad. I closed my eyes, imagining what would happen. Mom would lean over and see our awesome collage, all heart-shaped and romantic. All her best memories would come flooding back in a wave of ooey-gooey emotions. She'd remember all the great times she'd had with Dad. The two of them kissing on the couch, while I sat gagging in the middle. That time they wouldn't stop snuggling on the Ferris wheel and, you guessed it, there I was, covering my eyes and doing my best not to throw up. They so totally loved each other, and thanks to The Plan, all the weirdness of the past five weeks would be forgotten.

Dad was probably walking over right now. He'd spot her, her pale pink hair all cute and pulled back behind her ears. He'd smile, and Mom would melt into a literal puddle because, come on, it was Dad. He'd see our Table of All Things Romantic, and then notice the flyer for the Bigfoot Ball, strategically placed at its center, and . . . WHAM . . . back together again!

I opened my eyes and realized that the silence had gone on for way, way too long. What was happening? Was Dad doing that silent cry thing because he was so moved by my fancy booth?

Then my heart clenched at the sound of Dad's gravelly voice. "Kat?" He sounded . . . I don't know . . . angry.

"Hey," Mom said, her voice small, flat.

"What are you doing here? I was supposed to be meeting . . . Oh."

"Yeah. Oh." Pause. I eased upward in my seat. "Come look at this," Mom said.

Despite Calvin's warning stare, I peeked over the menus.

Mom and Dad had their backs to me. They were looking at the secret booth, at the heart poster, the photos, all of it.

This was it.

The moment all my hard work would pay off.

He would ask her, and Mom would say yes, and then . . .

"How's Gavin?" Dad said, his voice taking on a jagged edge.

Mom didn't answer. She turned her back on the photos, picking more furiously than ever at her fingernails.

"Did you have to bring him here? To Tanglewood?"

"Reed, please."

"I saw him, you know? At the freakin' grocery store. Shouldn't you two be back in New York by now? That's what you always wanted, right? To leave. So why don't you just leave?" My muscles seized up a little more with each word. I couldn't believe it. This wasn't happening. Dad had never shouted a day in his life. Sure, he yelled at the TV or at people in traffic, but never like this. Never like he really meant it.

"You know why I came back."

"Oh yeah? Then why won't you even talk to her? She's scared. She needs . . ." Dad stopped. I knew why he stopped, but I didn't want to see. I couldn't look away. There was Dad, working his jaw back and forth, doing his best not to cry out of sheer frustration, because that's what Dad did. Any time he got frustrated or sad or a little emotional, he'd break out in these tears you didn't expect, and then he'd be all embarrassed after, but there was nothing he could do to stop it.

I watched Dad trying not to cry, and I watched Mom standing there, not knowing what to do. And I watched Merline watching both of them from behind the counter, eyes wide.

"I'll come by tonight," Mom said. "I promise."

She reached out and tried to touch Dad's arm, but he pulled away. He buried his head in his hands, his shoulders all hunched up, and I could tell that Mom wanted to help him. Why didn't she? Normal Mom would have hugged him or said something to make everything okay.

"I'll see you later." Her voice cracked, like she had trouble getting out the words. "Around seven?"

Dad didn't answer. Mom stood there awhile longer, picking at her nails, and then she shook her head and walked around him, all the way around him like it would be the worst thing in the world if they accidentally touched. I sank back in my seat, my whole body numb.

The bell jangled, and just like that Mom was gone.

I looked over at Calvin, and he looked back at me. I expected him to say "I told you so" or something else totally annoying, but he didn't. He just blinked at me awhile, his eye feelings full of understanding, and then looked away. We waited for the bell to jangle a few more times, so we could be sure that Dad was gone.

Once enough time had passed, and the worst of the numbness had faded, we lowered our menus.

Dad was sitting right there on one of the stools at the counter. He gave me a sad little nod.

"That seat taken?"

I shook my head. He sank into the booth next to me, resting his forehead in his hands. "I like what you did with the pictures. You made it look real nice."

I didn't say anything. We sat there in silence for a while, and then Calvin slid out and said he had to go to the bathroom.

"I guess you heard. About Gavin?" Dad hung his head till his hair was brushing the table. "Sorry, baby. I didn't want you to see me like that."

Thoughts were racing through my head, but mostly my brain had gone blank. A big, frozen ball of nothing, and I was pretty sure I couldn't take any more huge revelations.

Dad let out a long breath and sat up a little straighter. He gave me a sideways glance. "They knew each other from before, from when she was a kid, then from art school. Her and Gavin." Dad couldn't stop the bitterness from seeping into his voice when he said the name. "Remember when she went back home for a week last year, to help her friend?"

I thought back to that week in November. Or was it December? Her friend's mom had died and she went up there to help out.

"That was . . . Gavin?"

"Yeah, but they weren't . . . you know. Dang, I shouldn't even be talking to you about this."

"Dad." He looked at me through bars of greasy hair, then went back to rubbing his face. "You have to tell me. It's way worse not knowing." *And if you tell me, then I'll know how to fix it.* Maybe. Although, honestly, my confidence had taken a huge blow the second Dad had said Gavin's name.

He thought on my words for a while. Calvin came over, hovered for a minute, then went back to clean up Operation Giant Failure.

Dad let out another breath that made his chest sink in on itself. "All right, here it is. She went to help him out, after his mom died. Like I said, they were friends, from way back, and that's all it was, but she never told me it was him. When I found out . . . I don't know, I kind of flipped. You were gone at that science thing, remember?"

The science club field trip. So it had been December. We'd stayed overnight at the Museum of Nature and Science in Dallas.

"And I was acting like a total jerk, yelling and accusing her of stuff she didn't do. And she left." Dad looked over at me again, like he was scared to see the expression on my face, but then his eyes relaxed. "She came back before you got home, but things were never the same after that. I don't know, maybe it's been a long time coming."

"But that was all the way back in December. And everything's been fine, until . . . art camp."

"You know that class we've been taking every Thursday? Ceramics or whatever?"

"Yeah, it was like date night, right? But you made pottery and stuff."

"We were going to this therapist guy," Dad said. "Couples therapy."

"But . . . you never told me. How could it be a long time coming when you never told me? And all the pictures. You always looked so happy." I could feel the stress and exhaustion of the past few days welling up in my throat, but I refused to let it show. Not now. I swallowed, hard. "You still love her, you said so."

"I do, baby. I always will, because she gave me you."

"Dad." The ache was building behind my eyes, but I kept right on swallowing. This wasn't happening.

"We decided to try some time apart. See how we felt. That's why she went to that camp."

"But you never said. You . . ." The cloud that sometimes followed me around settled on my shoulders, choking out my words.

Dad worked his jaw back and forth, rubbed his forehead. "I knew Gavin was gonna be at that art camp. I knew they had a . . . history. We never had too much in common, me and her. Not when it comes right down to it. Not till we had you, that is." He looked over at me, eyes shining, then back at the table. "But her and Gavin. They're both artists. He lives in New York City, where she's from. Has his own gallery and stuff where she could show her art, do what she really loves. They're just . . . you know . . . I get it. I really do."

I waited for Dad to say more, but I guess he had run out of words too. His body deflated till his face was basically melting into the table. I couldn't stand to see him that way.

I gave his big mermaid arm a hug, and that opened the floodgates.

Merline came over and then turned right back around when she saw us. She wasn't one for mushy emotional displays, at least not of the snot and tears variety.

"I'm supposed to be taking care of you, babe, not the other way around," Dad said, his voice all shaky and weak.

"You are, you're—"

Yeah, I couldn't finish. I guess I take after Dad in the whole getting-carried-away-with-my-emotions department.

When we'd finally gotten it all out, we emptied half the napkin dispenser to dry off and found Calvin, sitting alone in our now cleaned-out Booth of Eternal Doom and Failure.

"You okay?" he said. I nodded, even though I had no idea whether or not that was true. The past few days had been an emotional roller coaster, and I was ready to get off for a while and just be a kid. That didn't mean I was ready to give up, not by a long shot. But I was ready to give my brain a break.

CHAPTER 10

LAST RESORT

Mom didn't come by that night. I tried not to let it get to me.

It helped that my brain was once again a heaping bowl of mush.

Calvin was a great distraction, as usual, and we spent most of the day building our own bigfoot statue out of beer cans and duct tape. Not planning or scheming or talking about what had happened. Dad helped, with the building and with emptying out more cans. Once we'd sweated all the liquid from our bodies and then some, we went inside and Dad made peanut butter, honey, and bacon sandwiches. I know how it sounds, but trust me, they're amazing.

After that, we played Monopoly, which always made me laugh, since Dad always ran out of money in the first ten minutes, and then it was up to me and Calvin to fight it out for the win. Calvin's mom came by to pick him up just after nine, and she and Dad spent a while talking outside on the front steps.

"Sorry about your plan," Calvin said as he put the last of the game pieces back in the box. We'd lost the actual pieces forever ago, so we played with pennies and stray LEGOs.

"Yeah, me too." It was the first time we'd talked about Operation Giant Failure all day. Suddenly, the ugliness of earlier came rushing back to me, and I was surprised I didn't melt into a puddle of slime right there on the carpet.

"I guess now we'll have this in common too," he said, picking at his shoelaces. "Hey, about the Bigfoot Ball, and what I said last night . . ."

He trailed off, but I wasn't really listening. He was so sure it was all over with Mom and Dad. True, things looked . . . well, awful at the moment. But that didn't mean it was over. Just because his dad was a total jerk who never called didn't mean my mom would turn out that way. My parents were nothing like his. Okay, so Gavin was a problem, but problems had solutions, right?

"I was thinking," Calvin continued, now tugging on the end of one lace. "Since we usually go to the Bigfoot Ball anyway to help out, maybe this year we could—"

"It's late." I stood up, suddenly brimming with a renewed sense of determination. Along with total, mind-numbing exhaustion, but mostly determination. "I should probably go to bed."

"Oh." Calvin's eye feelings were all over the place, but mainly he looked hurt. "But it's only nine o'clock."

"Yeah, but your mom's here, and I guess I'm tired after Operation Giant Failure and everything."

"Right." He stood up, his long legs shaky after all that sitting.

"Sorry, I just can't really focus on ball stuff right now."

"Oh, okay. Forget I said anything." He hurried out, leaving the door hanging open behind him.

Usually, I would have gone after him, but in that moment I was happy he was gone. Calvin didn't understand. He couldn't. His parents had gotten divorced, and he hadn't done anything to stop it. Well, that wasn't me. I was Action

Girl. True, my first three plans had been complete and utter failures. But that's where the power of positive thinking came in. Failure wasn't the end. It was the first step on the road to success. I think I read that in a book once. It might be super cheesy, but it's also super true.

At least I hoped it was.

Later that night, lying on my carpet again, listening to the faint thud of june bugs bumping against my window, I started to formulate a plan. A New-and-Improved, Guaranteed-Not-to-Fail plan.

These were the facts I had so far:

Dad still loved Mom, but he was mad about Gavin.

Mom had more in common with Gavin, and he lived in New York where all the art stuff was.

Mom and Dad both loved me, and I wasn't the reason for the divorce.

The reason was . . . complicated.

Sigh.

That word again. Why did everything in life have to be so darn complicated? Why couldn't love be simple, like a recipe? Add these specific ingredients, in these exact amounts, and voilà! Love!

Reminding Mom how much she loved Dad hadn't

worked. Even if she did still love him, deep down, Dad was too angry about Gavin to see it.

My pen hovered over my Notebook of Extreme Awesomeness, but the ideas refused to flow. There had to be something. A way to fix the divorce and get Mom and Dad back to the way they were. *But it's been a long time coming, remember?* that creepy, naggy voice cooed in my ear. *Maybe Calvin's right. There's nothing you can do to fix it.* My inner voice devolved into fits of evil laughter, which was so totally not cool.

I opened up my laptop and clicked on Hi-hi!, waiting for the reassuring whoosh. I wasn't expecting JUNIEPIE28 to appear right away—did I mention she'd been pretty annoying so far?—but this time she did. Maybe she wasn't such an ultra-annoying person after all.

A new message box popped up with a ping.

JUNIEPIE28: Hey, kid, you still awake? What am I saying? Of course you are. You must be exhausted after the whole Operation Failure thing though. How you holding up?

I stared at her words for a minute before answering. She was me, right? So I shouldn't be surprised that she knew everything about me. Still, creepy. But I needed her. If anybody could give me insight into Mom and Dad, it would be Future Me.

BIGFOOT_GRL: How did you do it?

My fingers tingled as I typed the words.

BIGFOOT_GRL: Deal with it all? The stuff with Gavin and Mom? Dad? I need to know how I can get them back together.

JUNIEPIE28: Whoa, hold up! No way, kiddo. What do I look like, the Psychic Network? We're operating in a purely spoiler-free zone here, and don't push it. I so have better stuff to do than talk to you right now.

BIGFOOT_GRL: Really? It doesn't seem like it. Besides, I need answers!!!

JUNIEPIE28: Wow, did I really used to be this snarky? And demanding. What's with all the exclamation points?

BIGFOOT_GRL: If you can't tell me anything, then why are you even here?

I pushed up to my elbows, glaring at the screen. Didn't she know how important this was?

JUNIEPIE28: Hey, I'm not the one who needs something. It's your magic laptop. You brought me here. And who said I was here to help?

BIGFOOT_GRL: Why are you here, then? To annoy me to death?

JUNIEPIE28: That's it. Logging off.

BIGFOOT_GRL: No, wait!

JUNIEPIE28: Why should I?

BIGFOOT_GRL: I'm sorry, okay. That's me apologizing. Happy?

JUNIEPIE28: Not really, but it's that time of the month. Hormones, barf. Just be happy you don't have to deal with any of that yet.

BIGFOOT_GRL: Oookay.

JUNIEPIE28: Sorry, TMI, right? I remember how I was back then about period stuff. Anyway, fellow traveler, like I said. Not here to help, exactly. I'm here to warn you.

Parts of my first conversation with JUNIEPIE28 filtered back through my memory. Her words were still fuzzy, all dull and blurred at the edges, but I remembered what she'd said about magic.

BIGFOOT_GRL: About using magic?

My fingers were tingling again. So. Totally. Creepy. But I was using magic right now, wasn't I? A laptop that let me talk to my past and futures selves? What else would you call it? Not to mention a painting that changed based on my mood. Another big check in the magic-is-real column.

The answer to my problems had been staring me in the face all along. I looked over at my huge planning notebook, at all the blank space and scribbled-out ideas. Maybe this was it. I'd tried every normal way to help Mom and Dad. Now it was time for a little—

JUNIEPIE28: DON'T EVEN THINK ABOUT IT!!! I know, look at me with all the exclamation points, but this is serious.

BIGFOOT_GRL: What? Why? You said it yourself, this is a magic laptop. Which means that all of those pink tags were telling the truth. Weren't they?

JUNIEPIE28: Pump the brakes, kid. Do you have to

be so you all the time? This isn't a game or something you can fix.

BIGFOOT_GRL: But why not? It could be.

JUNIEPIE28: No! It can't!

BIGFOOT_GRL: You saw the stuff at that weird shop! If it's real, then there's a chance they have something there that could help.

JUNIEPIE28: N. O. As in no! As in this is a TOTALLY TERRIBLE idea!

BIGFOOT_GRL: What do you know anyway? It's not like . . . wait a minute. If you're trying to warn me, then that means you went back! To the shop! You used the magic too, so why shouldn't I?

JUNIEPIE28: Hello, older and wiser over here! Do you even understand the concept of a warning?

BIGFOOT_GRL: But you did go back?

I watched the dots scrolling at the bottom of the screen. I was sitting bolt upright now, waiting for her answer.

JUNIEPIE28: Fine, I went back, and that's why I know that you shouldn't. Magic is dangerous. It might seem like the answer to all your problems, but it's so totally not.

BIGFOOT_GRL: But why? If you're so stuck on playing Warning Girl, then give me details. What did you try, exactly? Did it make things worse?

JUNIEPIE28: No and no. I'm here to warn you, not give you tips on world destruction. Listen to Calvin. It's shocking, I know, but he's actually right on this one.

BIGFOOT_GRL: Right? He wants me to give up. That is SO not happening. Are you sure you're me?

JUNIEPIE28: Look, I know how you feel. It sucks, big-time. Like Mom and Dad are dropping a bomb on your perfect little vision board future, and there's nothing you can do to stop it.

BIGFOOT_GRL: How can you tell me to sit back and do nothing?

JUNIEPIE28: It's not about doing nothing. It's about accepting that there are some things in life you can't change. Setting goals is one thing. You make a list, mark things off. You do a bunch of tasks in the right order, and hey, you get what you wanted. This is different. Getting two people to stay in love . . . it's not about lists.

BIGFOOT_GRL: Okay, I get it. No more lists. That's why I need something else. That's why I need magic.

She didn't answer right away. I couldn't understand her, I mean me. Wow, this could get really confusing really fast. But why was she being like this? So what, magic was dangerous, but did she really expect me to give up on Mom and Dad?

BIGFOOT_GRL: Please, all I'm asking for is a little help.

JUNIEPIE28: Sorry, no can do, so you might as well stop asking.

I stared at the screen. Why was Future Me trying so hard to ruin my life?

JUNIEPIE28: Sigh. Don't be mad, okay?

JUNIEPIE28: Double sigh. Maybe it doesn't matter anyway. What is it they always say? The past is doomed to repeat itself? But hey, I had to try. I just hate to see you go through all that. Again.

BIGFOOT_GRL: Go through all what?

JUNIEPIE28: Spoilers! Jeepers, I'm giving you an F in the listening department.

BIGFOOT_GRL: Hey!

JUNIEPIE28: Sorry. Look, clearly you're going to go all Magicville, and there's nothing I can do to stop you. But let me give you one piece of advice, okay? Watch out for

The screen started to flicker, bolts of green lightning breaking apart the image.

BIGFOOT_GRL: Hey! Hello? Watch out for what?

The keyboard whirred and clicked, sending up tiny puffs of smoke. There was a pop, more smoke, and the screen went black.

No! My laptop!

I blew away the smoke and was surprised to find that the keyboard wasn't even hot. I pressed the on button, praying under my breath, and the screen instantly came to life. Like it had just been sleeping. Everything on the desktop looked normal, the pictures, the shortcuts. Hi-hi! was still open, but the chat box with JUNIEPIE28 had disappeared.

CHAPTER 11

JUST LIKE MAGIC

I didn't remember falling asleep, but I woke up to bright bars of sunlight burning my eyes. My body was one big ball of aches and pains and sweat. Don't forget about the sweat. It was at least a million degrees in my room, especially in the square of fiery sunlight I'd chosen for a bed.

I sat up, rubbing the sweat from my eyes, and that was when I saw the time. Eleven thirty in the morning. Seriously?

My head had that full feeling, like when you have a cold, but I wasn't sick. Just tired and sore and a little out of it. I still remembered the chat from the night before. All the gory details. Well, most of them anyway. I felt a little silly for all that magic talk. Despite a zillion pieces of evidence to the contrary, I still had a hard time believing The Shop of Last Resort actually dealt in magic. But still, I had to try.

I checked Hi-hi!, just in case. Nothing from Calvin, which was okay by me, because I still wasn't sure I was ready to talk. There was one message, though, straight from Magicville.

JUNIEPIE15: Good morning, sleepyhead! Rise and shine.

JUNIEPIE15: Did you work everything out with Mom and Dad?

JUNIEPIE15: I was right, wasn't I? You were just being a big poopy head. Mom and Dad are so totally lovey-dovey now, huh?

I didn't have the heart to tell her the truth. Past Me was so naive, as in totally clueless, while Future Me was this super-annoying ball of negativity. What was that all about?

BIGFOOT_GRL: Don't call me poopy head!!!

BIGFOOT_GRL: But yes, they're definitely still in love.

Or at least they would be. With that, I shut my laptop and put my most daring plan yet into action. Not that I had much to go on. My plan was to head back to The Shop of Last Resort and search for something, anything, that might help Mom and Dad.

First, breakfast. Dad was already at the table, serving up more heaping plates of bacon and eggs. He looked like a shaggy dog that had spent all night out in the cold and rain. Poor guy. I did my best to cheer him up, but bigfoot jokes can only go so far.

By the time I rode off on my bike, leaving him to work on Honey Pie by himself, he was still half man, half world's saddest rain puddle. Seeing him like that, all depressed and droopy, just added to my resolve.

I pumped my legs harder and harder, doing my best to outride the feeling that my new plan, if you could even call it a plan, was doomed. Magic? Seriously? That was the answer to all my problems? The certainty of the night before not only faded as I rode into a wall of muggy heat, it straight-up evaporated. What was wrong with me? Okay, the painting had been a little weird, but they could make holograms with phones now, right? Who was to say they couldn't design pictures that changed based on your mood using super-tiny computers?

And the laptop? Maybe it wasn't so much magic as it was me, sitting alone in my room, talking to myself. Maybe what I needed was a psychiatrist, not a trip to some "magical" tourist trap?

My wheel hit a rock, and I had to jerk the handlebars and do some fancy pedal work to keep from falling. Downtown was just around the corner. I could already see the tops of the colorful shops, stacked up all hodgepodge, and the foot poking out above the bigfoot tour bus and the . . . garden gnome floating through the twisting chimneys, his stomach swollen like a balloon, shouting curses at the people down below.

Wait. What now?

I skidded around the corner, tires hopping as the street changed from smooth asphalt to bumpy cobblestones. A boy of maybe five or six raced past, eyes wide and scanning the rooftops.

"Gomo! Come back! I didn't mean to make you fly away!" Before he turned the corner, I caught a glimpse of a plastic balloon pump gripped in one chubby fist.

"Curses on you and all of your kin!" shouted Gomo in response as he bounced down the sloping roof of A Yeti Sits Down for Tea.

My first instinct was to follow—hello, talking garden gnome!—but a group of tourists nearby exploded in fits of laughter. It was the hold-your-belly, try-not-to-snort kind of laughter. I climbed off my bike and stepped closer. They were all wearing pairs of ridiculous oversized glasses, just like the Laugh-o-Matic specs from The Shop of Last Resort.

Okay, this was all way too weird.

As Gomo's cries retreated into the distance, I left my bike in its usual spot outside The Friendly Bean and headed toward the shop. It should have taken no time to get there, since it was just around the corner, but the streets were packed full of people. And not just the ordinary bigfoot tourists with their cameras and fanny packs. All kinds of people buzzed around Main Street, most of them huddled in clusters, whispering over some strange object sporting a familiar pink tag.

What was going on?

I pushed my way through a group of kids holding a broken retainer up to the sunlight. "Try it," one of them said.

A girl with cool purple braids snatched the retainer and stuffed it in her mouth. A moment later, she spat out a dozen Hershey's Kisses, thankfully still in the wrappers, and the other kids dove to claim their sticky prizes. Gross.

The alley leading to The Shop of Last Resort was just as dark and chilly as I remembered, except now it was crawling with people. They milled here and there, chatting excitedly and showing off their latest purchases.

"The tag says it can make nose hairs disappear!" squealed a round woman holding up what looked like a broken toothbrush.

"They make every song sound like death metal," said a kid around JUNIEPIE28's age, dangling a pair of earbuds from his black fingernails. "How rad is that?"

This was all so totally not happening.

Except it was. All around me, strangers and people I knew from town were oohing and aahing over their latest discoveries. I squeezed my way inside and gasped. If the shop had seemed packed before, now it was practically overflowing. Every inch of the tiny shop was crammed with people grabbing for any item they could find.

And that wasn't the worst part. The shelves were almost empty.

I pushed into the nearest opening and fumbled for something, anything that might help. A group of bigfoot tourists had gotten there first, though, and I watched as they snatched up a bent spoon, a bag of old batteries, and a broken pen.

No! I couldn't read the pink tags, but they had to do something. Maybe they could have helped.

I tried again, turning around and diving into a gap in the crowd. I couldn't see through all the butts and fanny packs, but my fingers felt along the empty shelf until . . . victory! I cupped something cold and metal in my fist.

Prize in hand, I fled to an empty space near the front counter to sit and examine my find. All around, people were shouting and pushing. A high-heeled shoe flew through the air and hit the bigfoot bus driver in the head. Things were really getting out of hand.

Carefully, I opened my fist to find . . . a broken Hot Wheels car. The pink tag read, "Spin the wheels and feel instantly carsick."

Seriously?

My heart sank to the floor. I watched it sitting there, all sad and oozing, throbbing out my final dying heartbeats. All around, the noise grew to a deafening pitch. The room started spinning. It wasn't just the magic or the fact that my world had literally turned upside down. It was the realization that maybe Calvin and JUNIEPIE28 had been right. There wasn't anything I could do. Magic, or at least something that looked a whole lot like magic, was real, but even that wouldn't help. Who wanted to make themselves carsick?

I let the toy car fall from my hand, where it plopped down right next to my heart. An old lady in silver yoga pants snatched it up—the car, not my heart—and that was that. Total plan failure. I told myself to get up and dive back into the fray. There were a ton of other mostly empty shelves I had yet to explore, but what was the point?

All this magic was small, silly. Turning a garden gnome into a super-angry balloon? Getting rid of nose hairs? Nothing here could help me with Mom and Dad. Suddenly, I was more tired than I'd been in my entire life, like an invisible vampire had come and sucked out my life force. Or maybe it was the fact that my heart was still sitting there bleeding on the carpet.

I started to push up to my feet, ready to make a break for the door, when a ball of patchy fur brushed past my arm. Yikes! It was Mr. Winkles, except his fur wasn't as patchy as it had been before. It had blossomed into a thick coat of black and orange stripes. He looked like a tiger, if the tiger was round and about the size of a beach ball. Weird, because I didn't remember him being so large the other day. And double weird, because his wrinkles were gone too, or maybe they were just hidden under all that fur.

"You'll have to excuse Mr. Winkles, hon. He doesn't know the first thing about personal space." Mag craned her bony neck down so that her nose was almost touching mine.

"Oh, um, hi there," I said. Can you tell at this point that my Freak-o-Meter was ringing to the max? No, not to the max. My Freak-o-Meter had exploded in some kind of earth-shattering nuclear blast, and now my brain really was a bowl of mush. As in literal mush. Because here's the thing. Mag's neck wasn't covered in green veins like it had been before. Her wrinkles, the ones that used to drip down her face like strips of human seaweed, had been sucked back into her cheeks. They were still there, sure, but she looked way less old. Or maybe it was just the light. As if.

"Is there something I can do for you, honeycakes?" she said in her sugary-sweet voice, ignoring the chaos going on all around. "You look like you're in search of something special, am I right? How about you come on into the back and tell me all about it?"

Her long, thin fingers played a tune on the beaded curtain leading into the Restricted Section. She offered a sweet smile, and I found myself standing up and following her through the softly tinkling curtain.

As soon as the beads settled behind us, a hush fell over

the small, cozy room. Like the beads formed a thick wall separating us from the sounds of the shop. The room was about the size of our kitchen at home, except nearly every inch was covered in thick purple fur, including the ceiling. The light came from three Chinese lanterns, each giving off a soft pink glow. There weren't any shelves like in the rest of the shop, just a long glass display case with a few dozen objects resting on purple velvet.

The glow of the lanterns illuminated the tags, but in this room they weren't pink, but silver. "For sickness," one said. "For prosperity in business," read another. Like in the main room, the tags were attached to ordinary objects: a burnt-out lighter, a dented bottle cap, an empty pack of chewing gum.

I watched Mag take a seat in a cushy purple armchair near the display case. "You look different," I said, my voice taking on an eerie faraway quality in the strange, furry room.

"Do I? Well, thank you very much, hon. It must be my new hairdo." She primped up her hair, which I now noticed was wound into elaborate, bouncy curls. It did look different from the other day, more white-blond than pure white, but that wasn't all. She looked younger, almost like a different person.

Mr. Winkles waddled over to her side, rubbing her shins and releasing a loud, motoring purr. And what was up with her cat? Hair like that would take weeks to regrow.

"Lil' Binky Winkles got a haircut too," she said, fluffing up his fur. "Perked him right up, didn't it? My Little Booboo Winkle Cuddle Puss." I stared, wide-eyed, as she nuzzled the puff ball she called a cat. "Now, let's get down to business, shall we?" She waved me closer, taking a key from a hidden pocket of her dress and unlocking the display case. "Tell Miss Mag how she can help. Can't keep my customers waiting too long."

I stepped forward, but my voice had gotten swallowed up by way too much weird. What was even happening? Had the whole town of Tanglewood Crossing gotten sucked into *The Twilight Zone* right along with me and Mom and Dad? Apparently, yes. Flying gnomes, anyone?

Deep. Calm. Breaths.

Okay, this was really happening. The important thing was to remember why I was here. This was for Mom and Dad.

Mag tapped her long pink fingernails impatiently on the glass. "Anytime now, hon. Don't mean to rush you, but it's getting wild out there."

"I need . . ." My voice cracked, but I pushed onward. "I need a love spell. A love . . . thing, whatever you call it. For my parents. So they won't get divorced."

"Ah, now we're cooking." Mag pushed up to her feet and lifted the top of the glass display like a lid. She propped it up and studied the items inside, kneading her way-less-wrinkly chin.

"Is this stuff really magic?" I said, letting out one of the zillion or so questions zinging around inside my head.

"'Magic' is a tricky word, now, don't you think?" she said, turning to me with a twinkle in her eyes. "People think it's all some big illusion. Smoke and mirrors. Well, to those people I say phooey! Real magic is all about energy. What I like to call the spark."

I watched as she lifted up a broken hairbrush, examined it, then laid it back down again. "Taking energy from one place and directing it to another place. It all takes energy, hon. Remember that. You can't do any real magic, no matter how big or small, without a little of that good sparkly stuff changing hands."

She leaned down and retrieved a small gold padlock, about the size of a bottle cap, with a matching key dangling by a piece of string. The key was bent, and the padlock all scratched up, but otherwise they looked totally ordinary.

"I think this might do the trick," Mag said, holding the lock up to the dim lights. The tag read simply, "For love," with no further instruction. I had a lock like that on one of my old diaries at home. How could something so normal help fix Mom and Dad?

"How does it work?" I said as Mag dropped the lock into my open palm. I was surprised by the weight of it. The metal sent cool shivers tingling up my arm and into my fingertips.

Mr. Winkles growled as Mag nudged him off her foot, and he stalked away, back through the clinking beads. I caught a glimpse of the utter chaos erupting in the shop beyond, then once again the room fell silent.

"It's always hard to say with the really powerful magic," Mag said, giving my arm a motherly pat. "But if I were you, I'd wait till they were in the same room to use it."

"'They' as in Mom and Dad?"

"That's right, puddin' cup. And don't be surprised if there are a few teensy-weensy . . . side effects. Like I said, magic takes energy, and all that energy has to come from somewhere." Her lips curled into a pretty smile. Her teeth looked different than the other day, whiter and more like real teeth.

She turned toward the beaded curtain, but I called her back.

"Wait, how do I use it? I don't understand."

"Put the key in the lock, hon. The rest should take care of itself. It might not happen right away, mind, but it'll happen."

"But—I didn't even pay you yet." My nonexistent heart sank as the words spilled from my mouth. The price. I hadn't even thought about what something like this would cost. Sure, the stuff in the rest of the shop was dirt cheap, but it was all nose hairs and balloon gnomes. Something this powerful would probably—

"Oh, go on, now. It's on the house. What kind of mean old lady would I be, charging you for a broken lock? Besides," she said, leaning in close, "seems like you really need it." She gave me a friendly wink and then shuffled me back through the curtain and into the fray.

It was all I could do to push my way out of the shop without getting trampled, squashed, or otherwise smushed.

I didn't stop moving till I'd made it all the way back to my bike. The streets were still packed with people laughing and whistling and chattering away about the new, totally wild shop. I slid the padlock into my pocket and took off, pumping and pedaling till I was back on smooth asphalt and far away from the crowd.

Pretty soon, the sounds of downtown had faded, and I was zooming down the same old streets filled with the same old people and the same old broken-down houses. Boy, it felt good to be heading home. It all looked so normal. My heart opened especially wide as I approached the gate to Tanglewood Village. Well, technically, the trailer park didn't have a gate, more of a chain-link fence with a big gap in it where they'd put the gravel road, but you get the idea.

As I wound around the dumpster, the padlock pressing into my butt cheek, JUNIEPIE28's words echoed in my head. "Magic is dangerous." After seeing the way people were acting in town, I was starting to believe her. But this was Mom and Dad we were talking about. If there was any chance it might work, even a small one, I had to try it.

JUNIEPIE15 would understand. She still remembered all the good stuff. Oh, like that time I accidentally spilled this huge soda on Mom's white sweater when we went out for a fancy dinner at Catfish Cabana. And she'd been all embarrassed and wanted to go home, until Dad took his soda and dumped it over his head, right there in the restaurant in front of everyone. Mom laughed so hard after that she couldn't stop snorting. I bet JUNIEPIE15 remembered.

And that's why I had to try the magic. Even if it was weird and dangerous and probably wouldn't even work.

I pulled to a stop in front of our trailer, greeted by the

gentle clinking of spoon wind chimes and the soulful clunk, clunk of Dad's beer bottle whirligig. The weirdness of downtown melted away as I spotted Dad up on the roof patching holes. The trailer always got holes anytime it rained, and sometimes just because. He waved me over. I climbed up, and we sat there for a while, legs dangling over the edge, drinking ice cold root beers from his mini cooler.

"What'd you get up to today?" he said, wiping the sweaty hair out of his face. "Causing trouble?"

"Yeah, pretty much," I said, leaning back and soaking up the sun. No way I could tell him about the lock or my secret plans. Like he'd even believe me. And, in an instant, my certainty about the whole magic thing started to fade again. It was like the farther I got from the shop or the laptop or whatever, the more ridiculous it all seemed. Sure, back in the shop there'd been no doubt that it was real. Half the town had seen Gomo the gnome floating down Main Street, but still. It was like I was living in two worlds. The weird, wild world of The Shop of Last Resort, and home. The trailer and Dad and, hopefully . . .

"Your mom's coming over for dinner tonight. For real this time." His eyes were two slits, fighting against the sun. "Thought about making spaghetti. How's that sound?"

"Sounds great." My hand went to my pocket, feeling the outline of the lock and key.

Dad's eyes got even thinner, and he held a hand up to block out the rays. "We need to talk through what happens next. Your mom . . ." He trailed off for a moment, and I could feel him studying my face. "Heck, she'll probably tell you herself tonight, but she got an offer to show at this gallery in New York in addition to Gavin's place. I guess it's one of them fancy, big-deal galleries. Not like the community center out here." He sighed, closing his eyes to keep them from watering. "It's not like she's going away forever. No matter what, she'll always be your mom. You know that, right? She'll always be here, even if she's not . . . here."

My mouth had gone dry. I closed it, trying to suck some moisture back into my tongue, but it wasn't working. "So she's moving away?" All the hope I'd built up on the ride home fizzled out. Magic? Seriously? What had I been thinking? This was real. It was Mom and Dad, and Mom was . . .

"That's what we need to talk about." Dad rubbed his eyes some more, letting his hair fall back in his face. "Sorry, I probably shouldn't have said nothing yet. I'd better let her explain."

He sat up and pulled me into a hug. It was nice, even if

he was extra sweaty. "I'm proud of you, baby. I'm so . . . Dang, sorry, no way I'm about to start crying again. Not today. I just want you to know that we're gonna get through this, yeah? Together."

We stayed up there awhile longer and ate a few cold sandwiches. Bacon and cheese this time, which was almost as good as bacon and peanut butter.

After that, I went inside to hang out in my room. I took the tiny gold lock from my pocket, holding it by the key and the little white string. If I put the key in the lock when Mom got home, would something magical really happen?

Earlier, I would have said, "Duh, of course," but now I felt silly just asking the question. When had I turned into such a skeptic? I was like all those people online who left mean comments on Gram's blog, saying that she was silly for believing in bigfoot. But those people only said that because they chose to ignore the evidence.

Was that me? And why did I feel like vampire bats had sucked out all my blood and now I was a floppy, totally exhausted husk? I lay down in my usual spot on the carpet and opened up Hi-hi!

CALTHEDESTROYER: Hi.

That was from hours ago. Then another from more recently.

CALTHEDESTROYER: Guess you're not answering.

I wanted to answer, I did, but a small part of me was still mad. Calvin didn't think I could do anything to stop the divorce. He was sending me all these bad, negative vibes, and what I needed was the power of positive thinking. Even if the whole magic lock turned out to be a bust, I could still do . . . something.

Ping.

JUNIEPIE15: Hi, it's me! How are you? I'm sooo bored. Can you talk?

Great, seven-year-old me. Then again, I technically didn't have anything better to do until Mom got home. Unless you counted brooding.

BIGFOOT_GRL: Sure. What's up?
JUNIEPIE15: Nothing. Oh, except Mom is painting a giant bigfoot on my wall, and a bunch of trees and leaves and forest stuff. It's going to look so cool!

Oh yeah. I'd forgotten that she'd painted the mural back in second grade.

BIGFOOT_GRL: Where's Dad?

JUNIEPIE15: Oh, he's watching the game. So totally boring. But he said I can throw Cheetos in his mouth during the commercials, so that will be fun.

BIGFOOT_GRL: Cool.

JUNIEPIE15: Hey, can I ask you a question? I mean, since you're all old now and stuff. What's it like?

BIGFOOT_GRL: I am not old!

JUNIEPIE15: Are too!

Sigh. She was so totally obnoxious. But the funny thing was, I could feel the last bits of tension from my wild afternoon melting away.

BIGFOOT_GRL: Fine, you win. I'm super old.

JUNIEPIE15: So . . . what's it like? Are Mom and Dad all weird and wrinkly now? Ooh, what about school? Do you have a boyfriend?!

BIGFOOT_GRL: Whoa, slow down. One question at a time.

BIGFOOT_GRL: No, I don't have a boyfriend! And since when did you start liking boys?

JUNIEPIE15: Gross! Who said I like boys?

BIGFOOT_GRL: You're the one who asked.

JUNIEPIE15: Okay, what about school? Is middle school way cooler than elementary?

BIGFOOT_GRL: Um . . . not exactly. It's kind of the same, I guess. Except the boys smell bad and everybody has zits.

JUNIEPIE15: Eww! There has to be something good. The future can't be all zits and stinky boys! What about Mom and Dad? Are they different now?

That was the question I'd been avoiding. No way I could tell seven-year-old me that her perfect parents were about to get a divorce. Well, unless I could stop it.

BIGFOOT_GRL: They're . . . you know . . . great. Mom has pink hair now. It's super cool. And Dad and I are almost done fixing up Honey Pie.

JUNIEPIE15: What? You still haven't fixed Honey Pie? But we've been working on her since forever.

BIGFOOT_GRL: I know, but some of the parts are expensive, and really hard to find . . .

JUNIEPIE15: Sigh, I guess. Don't you have any good news? I mean, pink hair is pretty cool. What kind of pink?

BIGFOOT_GRL: Cotton candy pink.

I tried to think of some good news to cheer up Baby Me, but nothing came to mind. Mom and Dad were getting a divorce. Calvin and I were fighting. Gram was in a nursing home and might never go bigfoot hunting again. In short, being twelve kind of sucked.

All those years spent planning for the perfect future, and this was where I ended up?

BIGFOOT_GRL: Ooh, Merline and Big Vic got married, and we got to be the flower girl at their wedding! That was pretty fun.

JUNIEPIE15: REALLY!!! That is so cool, and romantic, and cool!

Jackpot.

JUNIEPIE15: What was the wedding like? Tell me everything!

I had started typing when I heard tires crunching over the gravel outside. I peeked through the blinds to see a shiny red hatchback pull up on the grass. The same car that I'd seen at the pond, parked at the front of the submarine.

The door opened.

It was Mom.

CHAPTER 12

BRAIN DRAIN

I went outside and there was Mom, leaning
against the red car, like everything was normal, looking like
a sad mermaid who'd spent way too much time on land. "Hi."
She held up her hand in a weak wave, and then came over to
hug me. I couldn't bring myself to hug her back. "Dad said
he made spaghetti. Are you hungry?"

"Sure, I guess." Yeah, as if.

I let her lead me to the trailer, even though the whole
time I wanted to shrug her arm off my shoulders. I could feel
the lock heavy and cold in my pocket. I looked back at the car
before we went inside, half expecting to see Gavin following

after us, rubbing his creepy little goatee, but it was just Mom.

In the kitchen, Dad was busy serving up heaps of wiggly noodles, a few stray ones clinging to his T-shirt.

"Jumped right out of the pot," he said, following my gaze. "Hey, baby. You wanna grab the sauce?"

"Sure." I was grateful for the excuse to move away from Mom.

Mom's phone rang, and she went outside to answer it. Dad spilled some more noodles and went in search of a paper towel. I stared down into the bubbling pot of tomato sauce, the red liquid popping and sizzling like lava.

"Be right back, okay? I think I've got some paper towels out in the truck."

I watched the door close behind Dad. The trailer had fallen silent, apart from the low burbling of hot liquid. This was it. I took out the lock and held it up to the light, letting the key dangle by the dirty string. How could something so ordinary change anything about Mom and Dad?

Short answer: It couldn't. Just like before with the laptop, my certainty about the shop and Gomo and all the wild customers had faded fast. Like a drawing on an Etch A Sketch. The image had been crystal clear at first, but the more I moved around, the more time I spent at home, the less real it seemed. The magnetic sand got all shaken up, and now it was just a big gray blur of fear and doubt.

But the laptop had turned out to be real. So why did this feel so different? So truly and utterly hopeless? Before, the lock had seemed like a lifeline, my one chance at fixing the divorce. Now it seemed pathetic and silly. My last hope? Seriously, self?

The front steps squeaked. Someone was coming inside.

With a long sigh, I slid the tip of the bent key into the lock. It would only go in halfway. Great, even that part didn't work. Oh well, what did it matter? Why had I ever thought that a broken lock would do any good? JUNIEPIE28 had been right. Things with Mom and Dad were complicated.

Still, she had tried to warn me.

That meant there had to be something to all this magic stuff, right? I scratched my head, more tired and confused than ever, and stuffed the lock back into my pocket.

The door opened. "Found 'em," Dad said, holding up the paper towel roll like a trophy. "All set with the sauce?"

He tossed me the paper towel roll, just like normal, and I caught it with one hand. "Yup, all set," I said, trying my best to sound cheery and not like the weight of the universe was slowly grinding me down into the carpet. Right along with those soggy noodles.

"Good deal, man. Let's eat."

Dinner was . . . tense. And not just because I was wait-ing to see what effect, if any, the lock had on Mom and Dad. Not that I was expecting much. By now, I was firmly stuck in gloom-and-doom, there's-no-way-to-fix-this mode.

Mom sat down in the middle of the nook like always, with Dad on her right and me on her left. That way, when she was done eating, she could scoot back into her corner and sketch. She liked to listen and observe, which worked out great, because Dad loved to talk. At least that's how it usually was.

Not tonight. Dad picked at his spaghetti, while Mom rolled her noodles into big knots on her fork, only to sit back and watch them unravel. I cut my meatballs into little pieces, resting my hand on the table between bites. True, I hadn't been sleeping much at all, but why was I so totally tired? And it wasn't normal tired either. It was like the tiredness had seeped into my bones and was dragging me down toward the table.

The longer we sat there, not talking, the deeper my heart dropped in my chest. Of course the magic hadn't worked. Sure, I thought I'd seen a bunch of strange stuff in town that afternoon, but what evidence did I really have? Gomo could have been a toy, a remote-control flying gnome designed to shout curses at people. And so some tourists had been laughing and talking about nose hair. So what?

And Mag? Mr. Winkles? Definitely creepy, but there could be a million explanations. As for talking to Past and Future Me, can you say "cry for help"? Even that part didn't seem real to me anymore. What if I'd made them up as some weird way to cope with the divorce?

Calvin had been right all along. There was nothing I could do to stop it. Mom and Dad would break up, and Mom would move away, and maybe, if I was lucky, I'd see her at Christmas.

"June?" Mom's voice cracked, breaking the silence. She sounded nervous, which was weird, because this used to be her home. It still was her home, right? She picked at her sea-green nail polish. "I know your dad talked to you about things, but . . . I wanted to see how you're feeling." She had her hair swept up in a pale pink ponytail that sat like a cuddly animal on the back of her neck. Her eyes looked so sad. Part of me wanted to reach over and take her hand, to stop her from looking so small and frail and alone, but the other, bigger part of me wanted to scream at her to go away. Because how did she think I was feeling? What kind of question was that? This whole divorce, i.e., the thing that was about to ruin my life, had been her fault.

"Sorry, silly question. I just . . . we need to talk about things." She put down her fork and slid a stray hair behind her ear. I watched her picking at her nails some more under the table. "About where you want to live."

"What?" I didn't intend to sound so mean, but the question took me by surprise. "I want to live here. At home. Where else?"

"No, of course, I . . ." Mom struggled to come up with the words. I looked over at Dad, but his eyes were locked firmly on his untouched spaghetti. "I know your dad told you that I got a gallery showing in New York, and that I plan to move there. We've talked it over and . . . we think it should be your choice. I know you love it here in Tanglewood Crossing, but there's a whole world out there, Junie. Whatever you decide, I want you to know that you'll always—"

"I'm staying here," I said, before she could even finish. "With Dad." The words cut into me the same way they cut into her—I could see it on her face—but they were true. And the reason they cut wasn't just because I was hurting Mom's feelings. It was also because Dad had given me a choice. How could he think that I would leave him here all alone? That I would abandon him to be with Mom . . . and Gavin?

"Okay, that's fine. I just wanted to make sure." Mom sounded defeated. Like a balloon after you pop it, when it's nothing but droopy plastic.

I didn't like to see her so sad, and all because of me, but I had to get out of there. The magic had given me hope, let me think that everything might be okay, just by sticking a key in some old lock. This was all way too . . . real. "Can I go to my room now?"

Dad finally looked up and nodded. I didn't even bother cleaning my plate before getting the heck out of Dodge.

I slammed the door to my room and collapsed facedown on the carpet. Maybe this was the new me. Twelve-year-old June, queen of darkness and brooding. Big ball of anger and destroyer of feelings. I turned on my old-school boom box so I didn't have to hear any more depressing conversations from the kitchen.

Once the heavy metal had soothed away some of my bad feelings, I got out the laptop. As soon as I touched the keys, my certainty about Past and Future Me came flooding back bit by bit. If the JUNIEPIEs were so made-up, some big emotional cry for help, then where did all the messages come from? Had I imagined them too? Because, yeah, I so totally hadn't.

So what about the lock and the other magical objects? Why couldn't my brain settle on a yes or no answer? The magic was real, or it wasn't. Simple, right? Apparently not so much.

Or maybe it was my fear talking. If the magic wasn't real, then . . .

Mom's face floated behind my eyes, and I could see the little lines at the edges of her mouth creasing with hurt. I didn't mean to hurt her feelings. It wasn't my fault that I was closer to Dad. Was it?

Hi-hi! started up with a whoosh. I saw a string of messages from Calvin, but didn't bother reading them. He wouldn't understand. If I even told him about the magic, he'd probably laugh in my face. Or maybe not. Whatever, I wasn't in the mood right now to argue.

Ping.

JUNIEPIE28: You went back, didn't you?

I stared at her words. Okay, so, that was a big yes on the magical laptop front.

BIGFOOT_GRL: Not like it did any good.

JUNIEPIE28: Oh, to be young and foolish again. Those were the days.

BIGFOOT_GRL: What's that supposed to mean?

JUNIEPIE28: Sigh. It means, you should have taken my advice. Magic, bad idea. Don't worry, I'm done yelling at you. I've had some time to think since we last talked.

BIGFOOT_GRL: Are we talking? Really?

BIGFOOT_GRL: I mean, it's weird. All this magic stuff keeps happening all around me, to me, but I can't bring myself to believe in it. One minute I do, the next minute it's like I forget it ever happened. Or not forget exactly, it just doesn't seem real anymore. Does that make any sense?

JUNIEPIE28: Totally and completely. It's the magic brain drain. Remember how I said my memories of that summer are all weird and fuzzified? I think it has something to do with how the magic works. When you're near it and it's working, you believe. When you get farther away from it . . . not so much. It's probably why so-called normal people act like such huge Muggles all the time. Even if they see magic happen, the certainty fades fast.

BIGFOOT_GRL: That actually makes total sense. How do you know all this stuff?

JUNIEPIE28: Well, to be fair, I wasn't always the wise, smoking-hot babe you find before you. I was you, remember? But don't worry, you'll get there one day.

BIGFOOT_GRL: Hey!

JUNIEPIE28: Chill. I'm just saying, I learned my lesson. About all of it. Magic, life, relationships, the whole shebang. Maybe you have to learn it too.

BIGFOOT_GRL: Meaning?

JUNIEPIE28: Meaning, all of my dire warnings might have been a little . . . melodramatic. Imagine that. Don't get me wrong! Magic is dangerous. Whatever you try will go horribly wrong, and you'll wish you'd never done it. But, like I said, here's me being older and wiser: Maybe that's a lesson you need to learn for yourself.

BIGFOOT_GRL: But the magic didn't even work.

JUNIEPIE28: Sigh, if only we had been that lucky.

JUNIEPIE28: Ugh, gotta go. The boyfriend can't figure out how earbuds work.

BIGFOOT_GRL: Does that mean it will work?

BIGFOOT_GRL: Hang on, did you say boyfriend?!?

JUNIEPIE28: Duh, learn how to read. Oh. My. God. You stick them in your ears! I swear, this boy.

BIGFOOT_GRL: Wait! What's going to happen?

JUNIEPIE28: Look, don't freak out, okay? It'll get bad, but you can handle it. I did. Oh, and talk to Calvin already. He's your best friend! And I seem to remember he wasn't always so completely useless.

BIGFOOT_GRL: Calvin?

JUNIEPIE28: Bye, Diaper Baby. BTW, not that you'll listen to me or anything, but watch out for the old lady. The formerly old lady, whatever. And the cat. Every time you use the magic, she's taking

Once again, green lightning bolts shot across the screen. The image distorted, the pictures on the desktop background twisting and flickering, until they came together to form a face. The face smiled, revealing smooth white teeth and golden hair, and then the laptop went black again with a puff of gray smoke.

CHAPTER 13

SECOND HONEYMOON

"The old lady's taking what?" I said aloud, blinking my eyes against the final wisps of smoke. I tapped the power button, and once again, the computer woke up. As if nothing had happened. I looked at the pictures in the background of me and Mom and Dad. I got a little pang in my stomach at the sight of Mom's face. After what I'd said earlier, did she think I didn't love her?

I opened Hi-hi! Of course, there was no sign of JUNIEPIE28. What had she been trying to tell me? I slumped back onto the carpet, closing my eyes, just for a second. The heat and the cushy carpet and the weight of all those questions closed in around me, like I was sinking into a giant feather pillow. I could hear the faint sounds of Mom and Dad outside, talking on the front steps.

I rolled over, trying to drag myself toward the blinds to get a look, but I was so . . . tired. Every muscle drooping downward. Maybe I could check on them in a few minutes. A few . . . But if JUNIEPIE28 was right, and something was about to happen, I had to . . . but first I would just rest my eyes for a few seconds . . . a few . . . a . . .

I woke up to the sound of Mom giggling. Rubbing the sleep from my eyes, I pushed up onto my elbows. What was happening to me? My muscles had turned to jelly, and it took every ounce of energy I had just to sit upright. I looked over at the bigfoot clock sitting on my dresser: 4:27 in the morning. Could that be right?

Another peal of laughter drifted down the hallway.

"Mom?" My voice came out gritty and weak, but that was definitely her laugh.

Gathering all my strength, I grabbed the edge of the bed and pulled myself to my feet. I so needed to get more sleep. Unless this was what JUNIEPIE28 had been trying to warn me about. I remembered what Mag had said, about magic being all about energy. First brain drain, now this. Total. Mega. Creepsville.

"Oh, Reed, that tickles!" Mom squealed from the living room. Okay, this was getting weird now. Energy drain or not, I had to investigate.

I reached down and felt the lock still secure in my pocket. Pausing at my bedroom door, I drew in a deep breath. Whatever was about to happen, I could handle it. JUNIEPIE28 had, and so could I.

Easing my door open, I peered into the living room. Mom was squirming on the carpet wearing her swimsuit, flippers, and orange floaties, and Dad was busy making kissy noises into her stomach. I watched as Mom dissolved into wild giggles, and Dad turned his attention to kissing her toes.

"Mom?" I said, stepping into the light of the living room. "You're still here." I'm not gonna lie, a wave of joy filled me up at the sight of Mom and Dad looking so happy, but it was also . . . weird. I could hear seven-year-old me gagging loudly in my ear.

Mom perked right up at the sound of my voice, but Dad kept on kissing Mom's toes, like he hadn't even noticed me. "Junie Pie, there you are!" she said, eyes sparkling, her smile wider than I'd seen it in years. "You'll never believe what's happened! It's so, so romantic! Your dad and I are going on a second honeymoon! Isn't it exciting?" She dissolved into laughs again as Dad licked the sole of her foot. Can you say gross much?!

"Oh, muffinbutt, not in front of June," Mom said, swatting Dad playfully with a beach towel.

Dad looked up, surprised, like he'd just now realized I was there. "Oh, right, sorry, kid." He crawled over to me, cheeks red, and that was when I noticed what he was wearing. Cargo shorts and a Hawaiian shirt. Seriously? That was so not Dad.

"We're going to the Bahamas, baby! Ain't that awesome?" Dad said, his eyes all wide and glazed over. He gave my shoulder a squeeze, then turned his attention to stuffing beach towels and sunscreen into his old gym bag. "Just like your mom always wanted. A real honeymoon. We kept putting it off for years, remember? Why'd we do that anyway? I mean, whatever my baby wants, my baby gets, am I right?" He dropped the gym bag and started making kissy noises in Mom's ear.

I stood there, openmouthed, watching Dad slobber on Mom's neck and Mom giggle so hard tears ran down her cheeks. Was this magic? The thing JUNIEPIE28 had warned me about? If so, it was . . . kind of amazing.

Right? Mom and Dad were happy again. Gross, definitely, but happy. No way they would get a divorce now. JUNIEPIE28 had been wrong. The magic worked great. Perfect, in fact. But I had to make sure.

"So, Mom, you're not moving to New York, then?" I said, the words heavy in my throat.

"What?" Mom gasped for air in between laughs, which was understandable because Dad was blowing raspberries into her stomach. "New York? What gave you that idea? New York's no place for a honeymoon. Sun and sand, that's what we need. Right, my little Reedy bear?"

"Right on, baby."

Mom attacked Dad's mouth and they were full-on kissing, rolling around in their beach clothes in the middle of the night, and it was so . . . totally great. It was exactly what I'd wanted.

"This is so cool," I said, talking loudly so I could be heard over all the smacking. "But how can we afford it? Isn't a trip to the Bahamas like super expensive?"

Dad came up for air long enough to say, "Who cares about money, babycakes, when you've got true love?" He flashed me a cheesy smile, before Mom covered his face in kisses.

Okay, time for a distraction. This was getting so totally

gag worthy. Planning! That could be my job. If I volunteered to help them plan the trip, then they'd have to stop kissing, right? At least for a few seconds.

"So when are we leaving?" I said, picking up a pair of goggles and a snorkel and stuffing them into Dad's bag. "We'll have to get passports, of course, which I think can take a couple weeks, and book flights and a hotel room and . . ."

Mom and Dad stopped kissing, turning to me with looks of childlike confusion.

"Hon, I thought you knew," Mom said, frowning. "We're leaving today! Ooh, that reminds me, what time is it?" Mom scrambled to her feet, which was hard since she was wearing flippers, and went over to look at the oven clock. "Four forty-five a.m., eep! We'd better go, pookums," she called over to Dad, who pried the bag from my grasp and hoisted it over his shoulder.

"Ready when you are, sexy mama," he said, shooting Mom that same cheesy smile and barely noticing I was there.

"You understand, right, Junie Pie?" Mom said, leaning down and patting my head like I was a puppy. "Your dad and I just need some adult time. But don't worry, we'll be home before you know it." She gave me a big kiss on the cheek then wrapped her arms around Dad.

"Let's hit the road, kitten!" Dad said, picking Mom up and carrying her to the doorway.

"Wait, what?" I said, my voice cracking as I followed after them. "You're leaving without me?"

Dad tried to squeeze Mom out sideways, but in the end he had to put her down.

"Bye, kid," he said, giving my shoulder a fake punch. "We'll send you a postcard, all right? You be good while we're gone."

"Love you!" Mom crushed me in a hug, and then they took off, running arm in arm to Dad's truck, Mom tripping every few feet on her flippers.

I followed, staring in disbelief.

"But you can't go!" I said as Dad loaded up the truck and Mom did a little happy puppy dance.

"Honeymoon! Honeymoon! Is there anything better than a honeymoon!" Mom sang, shaking her flippers, and then she climbed into the truck after Dad.

"Wait!" I called, running up and trying to pry open Dad's door. "What about me? You can't just leave me here!"

"Don't worry, hon," Mom said from the passenger seat. She stuck out her bottom lip, talking in a baby voice she had never once used in real life. "You'll meet someone one day.

Then you can have your own honeymoon and be as happy as me and your dad."

"That's right, baby," Dad said, reaching down to pat my shoulder, his eyes all shiny and strange. "Besides, we'll be back in two weeks. You won't even notice we're gone."

"But Dad, you can't! You can't go!"

Before I could even finish, Dad had cranked the engine. I grabbed for his mermaid tattoo, but he shrugged me off, punching the gas and speeding away with a rattle and a blast of smoke. I watched, body sagging, as Dad's old truck bumped down the gravel road and out of sight.

Moving like I was in a dream, I made my way back toward the trailer and sank down on the front steps. Everything JUNIEPIE28 had said turned out to be true. The magic had been real after all, and it had gone horribly wrong. Mom and Dad loved each other again, which was what I'd wanted, but they didn't love me. Not really. An ache opened up in my stomach, like someone had scooped out my insides, turning me into the world's saddest jack-o'-lantern, empty and alone.

Hand shaking, I removed the lock from my back pocket. How could something so simple have changed everything? Heat hardening in the back of my throat, I grasped the key and wrenched it out of the lock.

I looked out at the yard, the tall grass blowing in the cool night breeze. I looked over at the moths and crane flies whispering against my window, drawn by the floodlight buzzing atop the roof.

Nothing happened.

Surely, removing the key would undo the magic, right?

I slumped down, muscles weaker than ever, like lumps of raw meat without any tendons or bones. My head settled against the cool metal door frame, eyes fluttering. If I just closed them for a few seconds.

"No!" I spoke out loud, because that was the only way I could stay awake.

I dragged myself inside, moaning with the effort, and collapsed onto the safety of my bedroom carpet. I would fix this. Undo it. I had to . . . fix . . . it . . .

CHAPTER 14

GONE GRAY

I woke up to ripples of sunlight washing over my skin. It was morning. My whole body was one big ball of sweat, and my head pounded. What was that noise? That awful ringing?

I rolled over, still groggy, and there it was again.

Not so much a loud ringing as a quiet ping.

The laptop stood open beside me, and I saw a whole string of messages from Calvin, starting from yesterday.

CALTHEDESTROYER: Hey. Sorry about what I said.

CALTHEDESTROYER: June?

CALTHEDESTROYER: Are you mad at me? I didn't mean it. Maybe you're right. Your parents are different. Maybe they'll stay together.

CALTHEDESTROYER: Are you there?

CALTHEDESTROYER: So, the Bigfoot Ball's tomorrow . . . and I wanted to ask you something.

CALTHEDESTROYER: Hello?

CALTHEDESTROYER: You know, you could at least answer me. I didn't do anything wrong.

CALTHEDESTROYER: June?

CALTHEDESTROYER: Whatever. Never mind. I'm going out.

There was a gap of a few hours, then Calvin came back. I guess the whole no-message-log thing only applied to magical conversations, not the average, Calvin-hates-me-now variety.

CALTHEDESTROYER: Hey, are you there?

CALTHEDESTROYER: I went back to that shop and it's, um . . . extra weird now.

CALTHEDESTROYER: Actually, I think I might have made a huge mistake. Sorry, someone's knocking on the door, I'll be right back.

CALTHEDESTROYER: June! Are you reading this? I definitely made a huge mistake!

CALTHEDESTROYER: This Girl Scout troop just broke into my house, and now they're banging on my bedroom door! They say they love me! They won't stop screaming and making kissy noises. It's really starting to freak me out!

CALTHEDESTROYER: Hold on, I'm gonna use my dresser to block the door.

CALTHEDESTROYER: Yikes! One of them's climbing the tree outside my window! Now she's pelting the glass with chocolates! Yuck, there's gooey caramel everywhere.

CALTHEDESTROYER: That's it, I'm hiding in the closet.

CALTHEDESTROYER: Okay, I think I'm safe.

CALTHEDESTROYER: Confession time, I got this magic thingy from that creepy shop lady. She said it was some kind of love spell for . . . well . . . you know, just because. I did exactly what she said, shook up the snow globe and thought of the person I . . . I mean, you know, I just shook up the snow globe, and now every girl I see is totally in love with me.

CALTHEDESTROYER: Like creepy, I'll-break-down-doors-to-get-at-you in love. June, I don't know what to do.

CALTHEDESTROYER: Oh no, I think they found a way in. This is so not good. I'm going to stop typing now so they don't . . . oh crud . . .

CALTHEDESTROYER: June, help!

By this time, my heart was beating into my throat. Calvin! The last message was just sent ten minutes ago. Maybe he was still okay. I started typing frantically.

BIGFOOT_GRL: Calvin, I'm so sorry! I just read your messages. Are you okay? Please tell me you're okay!

I waited, not breathing, heart pounding in my ears. Finally, the three blinking dots appeared.

CALTHEDESTROYER: June! It's you!

BIGFOOT_GRL: It's me. ☺ Are you alive?

CALTHEDESTROYER: I think so . . . barely. Kidding, I'm fine. I mean, it got pretty sticky there for a second.

BIGFOOT_GRL: OMG, what happened?

CALTHEDESTROYER: So you believe me about the whole magic thing?

BIGFOOT_GRL: Unfortunately, yes. It's been a weird night.

CALTHEDESTROYER: Thank goodness. About you believing me, not the weird night. Yeah, so I did this whole love spell thing, and it went totally wrong. The Girl Scouts broke into my room and started attacking me. Then, thankfully, one of them knocked the snow globe from my hands and it broke.

CALTHEDESTROYER: After that, they all just looked around, dazed, like they didn't even remember how they'd gotten there. It was . . . awkward. Then they sort of just wandered off.

BIGFOOT_GRL: Seriously? So breaking the snow globe stopped the spell?

CALTHEDESTROYER: Yeah, I guess.

An inkling of hope blossomed in my chest. Maybe taking the key out of the lock had worked after all. Or maybe I should find a way to destroy it for good. I sat up straighter, thinking of ways I could melt metal, when another thought occurred to me.

BIGFOOT_GRL: Wait, so why'd you try a love spell in the first place? You said there was nothing you could do to get your parents back together.

CALTHEDESTROYER: True . . . and I'm sorry if I made you mad, I was just being honest.

BIGFOOT_GRL: But that is why you did the spell thing, right? To get your parents back together. Only it backfired?

CALTHEDESTROYER: Oh, that. Yeah . . . right. That's why I did it.

I was telling Calvin all about my magic gone wrong when I noticed a familiar sound coming from nearby. It was like a cross between a freight train and a pig blowing bubbles underwater. Snoring! But that could only mean . . .

I lunged for the blinds and peeked outside. My heart— boy, that thing had been through a lot lately—soared in my chest. Dad's truck was parked on the grass outside. He was back! Which meant that maybe taking the key out of the lock had worked after all!

BIGFOOT_GRL: Cal, gotta go check something. Be right back.

CALTHEDESTROYER: Wait! Look in the mirror first.

BIGFOOT_GRL: What?

CALTHEDESTROYER: Just do it.

I looked in the mirror hanging off my closet. Holy. Crab cakes! A long streak of white ran through my otherwise-brown hair. I trailed the strange, colorless strand through my fingertips. It felt normal enough, but . . .

BIGFOOT_GRL: What is that? My hair's gray! Or white or whatever! How did that happen?

CALTHEDESTROYER: I'm pretty sure it's the magic. I think that lady, Mag, is doing something to everyone who uses it.

JUNIEPIE28's warning. She's taking . . . what? Energy? Life force?

CALTHEDESTROYER: We have to stop her.

BIGFOOT_GRL: You're right, I . . .

The snoring stopped suddenly, and I heard Dad groaning.

BIGFOOT_GRL: Cal, I'll be right back. Promise.

I pulled on my BIGFOOT LIVES hat to cover my white streak, and then rushed to Dad's room as fast as my tired legs would carry me.

"Dad?" I knocked once, listening. "Is that you?"

I waited. The mattress squeaked. "Ouch!"

"Dad? Are you okay?"

The door cracked open, and there was Dad, hair wild, face crumpled with the imprint of his blanket. He rubbed the grit from his eyes. "Sorry, baby, I hit my foot on something. What time is it? I feel like I got run over by a truck."

I looked behind him at the mess of beach towels and flip-flops on the carpet. He'd probably hit his foot on Mom's hair dryer, which had spilled from his gym bag, along with bottles of sunscreen, goggles, and other beach gear. He followed my gaze, his forehead scrunching up into one big frown. He rubbed his eyes again, like he couldn't figure out what he was looking at. "What's all that stuff doing out? You planning a trip I don't know about?"

"No . . . You don't remember?"

He turned to me, dragging a hand over his forehead. "Remember what? Going on a beach vacation? Nah, I don't think I'd forget something like that. Last thing I remember, your mom went home, and I went to bed. After that . . ." He trailed off, the frown between his eyes deepening. "I don't know. Went to sleep, I guess," he said, not sounding too sure. "But what's all this stuff doing here?"

"Oh . . . that." I racked my brain, trying to come up with an answer. "I thought maybe you and I could go to the lake this weekend. I mean, if you want to."

"Yeah, sure, baby," he said, giving my shoulders a big squeeze. He wasn't wearing his Hawaiian clothes anymore, thank goodness, but I spotted them crumpled up in the corner.

"So Mom went back to the submarine?" I said, while Dad went in the bathroom to brush his teeth.

"Yeah," he said, his voice all warbly with toothpaste. "Hey, about last night . . ." He spat, and then peeked around the corner, a glob of toothpaste clinging to his chin. "You know I'd never want you to move away, right? Without you this place would be, I don't know, just some old, nasty trailer. But you're not a kid anymore, you know? I thought you should be able to decide for yourself."

"I know." I could feel the tears building up behind my eyes, because even if I did know, maybe I needed to hear him say it. I swallowed hard, forcing the tears back down again. I'd had enough crying for one lifetime.

"How about some breakfast? You in the mood for pancakes?"

"Yeah, sure."

"Nice, let me get the griddle going."

"I just need to talk to Calvin real quick first. Online. He had some weird stuff happen last night."

"Oh yeah, he all right?"

"Fine. I think everything worked out for the best."

"Awesome. Pancakes ready in ten. Don't be late."

I hurried back to my room and Calvin.

BIGFOOT_GRL: Guess what? Dad's back! And he doesn't remember anything about last night.

CALTHEDESTROYER: That's good, right?

BIGFOOT_GRL: Totally!

Even as I sent the message, my heart deflated a little in my chest. I was relieved that Dad was home and back to normal, big-time, but it didn't change anything about the divorce.

Mom was still moving away to live with Gavin, barf! I looked at my vision board, forgotten in the corner of my room. The edges had curled over and started to yellow in the sunlight. It was weird to think that pretty soon I wouldn't have any new pictures with Mom, except maybe from Christmas or my birthday. If she decided to show up next year, that is.

CALTHEDESTROYER: Back to what I said before. Are you in?

BIGFOOT_GRL: In?

CALTHEDESTROYER: Yeah, with stopping Mag? I mean, I don't know for sure how she's doing it, but she's definitely feeding on people somehow.

BIGFOOT_GRL: It's so creepy! And did you see her face? And Mr. Winkles?

CALTHEDESTROYER: I know! Remember Skyler from across the street? That kid with green hair? Well, yesterday, I saw him buy a broken skateboard from the shop, and now his green hair's gone completely gray. It's like she's getting younger, while everybody who uses the magic gets older.

BIGFOOT_GRL: She's like some weird retail vampire, yikes!

CALTHEDESTROYER: So, you're in?

BIGFOOT_GRL: Definitely. But what can we even do?

Calvin was right. There was no more room for me to question whether or not the magic was real. Dad almost leaving me to go to the Bahamas had proven that. And the white streak in my hair, not to mention my total exhaustion, proved that something weird was going on with Mag. We had to act fast, but how?

CALTHEDESTROYER: Oh . . . I was kind of hoping you'd have a plan. You are Action Girl, right?

Usually, that was true. Any other day, I'd have whipped out my trusty notebook and been halfway through the let's-defeat-Mag to-do list. Today, it was all I could do to stay awake. Not to mention the fact that my mind was still locked on Mom and Dad.

BIGFOOT_GRL: Not so much at the moment. I'm still distracted with the whole my-life-is-totally-over thing.

CALTHEDESTROYER: Oh yeah, that. Sorry, I should have realized.

BIGFOOT_GRL: But I still want to help. Maybe we should just go over there.

CALTHEDESTROYER: To the shop?

BIGFOOT_GRL: Yeah, you know? Go undercover, see what we can see.

CALTHEDESTROYER: I like it. Action Girl comes through yet again!

BIGFOOT_GRL: It's not exactly a plan.

CALTHEDESTROYER: Close enough. Meet you at the shop in an hour?

BIGFOOT_GRL: Sure thing!

CALTHEDESTROYER: June? Are you still there?

BIGFOOT_GRL: Yup. I have to go eat pancakes in a sec though, so I don't have long.

CALTHEDESTROYER: Did you get a letter in the mail from me?

BIGFOOT_GRL: What? Like a paper letter?

CALTHEDESTROYER: Yeah. It's no big deal. I sent you this letter, and . . . anyway, I wanted to say that when you get it, you should just throw it away. The stuff I wrote is really embarrassing and . . . I don't know . . . I kind of sent it by mistake.

BIGFOOT_GRL: How do you send a letter by mistake?

CALTHEDESTROYER: Um . . . I . . . I didn't send it by mistake exactly. What I mean is, just don't open it, okay? Promise?

For some reason, my heart was doing these weird little flip-flops in my chest.

CALTHEDESTROYER: June?

BIGFOOT_GRL: Yeah, sure. I promise.

Now with one more thing to puzzle over, I headed into breakfast. Dad had made enough pancakes to feed every tourist in Tanglewood Crossing and then some. He heaped a huge stack onto my plate and doused it with syrup.

"I wonder if Gavin remembers to add cinnamon to his pancakes, the way your mama likes," he said as he dropped down into his seat, crushing the air from his rubber butt cushion. He looked over at me, then got all ashamed of himself, letting his hair drop into his face. "Sorry, I shouldn't be saying that stuff in front of you. I'm sure Gavin's a real nice guy." Every time he said Gavin's name, it looked like he'd accidentally swallowed a mouthful of lemons and was doing his best to get rid of the taste.

"Don't worry, I hate him too," I said, and that made Dad burst out laughing so hard he knocked over his orange juice.

Dad and I understood each other. Gavin was the problem here. If only there was a spell that could make it so that Gavin had never been born. That was the kind of magic worth going gray over.

"Nice hat," Dad said, taking a huge bite of pancakes that barely fit on his fork.

"Thanks, I didn't feel like washing my hair." I checked to make sure the white strand was still securely in place.

"Me neither," he said through a mouthful of pancake, shaking out his greasy mane. Dad could be super funny, and smelly, but mostly hilarious.

After breakfast, I helped Dad clean up, which included freezing about a zillion leftover pancakes, and then asked if I could go meet Calvin.

"Sure thing, honey pie. Think you'll be back for lunch? Thought I might heat up some pizza."

"Maybe," I said, feeling bad for leaving Dad all alone when he was feeling so down in the dumps. "I'll try."

"All right, baby. Don't do anything I wouldn't do."

"Bye, Dad."

At the last minute, I decided to stick the laptop in my backpack, even though it was super heavy. JUNIEPIE28 hadn't shown up during my conversation with Cal, but if we needed help with Mag, she'd be the one to ask.

A cool breeze greeted me outside as I climbed onto my bike. That was so not like the usual muggy heat of Tanglewood Crossing. I looked up to see a wall of gray clouds rolling in over the mountains. Somehow, it seemed fitting.

I made my way toward downtown, scenes from the past few days playing over and over in my head. Dad climbing out of his truck, saying, "Honey pie, we need to talk." Gavin coming out of the silver submarine when I was supposed to be talking to Mom. "Oh dang, is this her?" Mom asking if I wanted to leave Dad and live with her. The look on her face when I said I didn't.

Everything was so weird and messed up. If only I could switch places with JUNIEPIE15. Go back to a time when stuff was simpler. Mom and Dad were in love, duh! Hello! A time when I didn't have any doubts or worries, except maybe why Mom and Dad wouldn't stop smooching whenever I tried to watch *SpongeBob SquarePants*.

The smooth asphalt turned to cobbles, and I climbed off my bike and left it leaning against The Friendly Bean, just like always. I'd forgotten that today was the day of the Lovers' Brunch, and after that, the Bigfoot Ball. Inside, couples were sitting at romantic booths, like the one I'd decorated for Mom, eating chocolate cake and sipping Merline's special Heartthrob Milkshakes. Later that night at the community center, they'd be dancing to sappy music, swaying and smooching and generally being ooey-gooey romantic.

But not Mom and Dad.

Calvin screeched to a halt, practically running me over. When he'd climbed off and stowed his bike next to mine, he came over to stand beside me.

"Guess you're not helping out with the ball this year?" he said, tucking a strand of gray hair into his MONSTER DELI ball cap.

I shook my head. "Too much going on."

"Yeah, that makes sense." He sounded kind of sad, which was weird, because Calvin had never been a huge fan of the ball.

"You ready for this?" I said, tightening the straps of my backpack.

"Ready as I'll ever be."

CHAPTER 15

CARVED IN WAX

As we made our way slowly toward the shop, I noticed something strange about downtown. "Are you seeing what I'm seeing?" I said, looking over at Calvin, who seemed to be reaching the same conclusion.

"The streets are empty. But yesterday—"

He was interrupted by Mrs. Emmeline Sweetie, owner of Sasquatch Sweeties, who hustled past, attempting to use a napkin to cover an explosion of gray hair. "This can't be happening. I'm too young for this, you hear me? Way too young! What will my sweet Bobby think when he sees me? Oh, deary me. This is a fashion emergency. Emergency, I tell you!"

She disappeared around the corner, still muttering to herself.

"We'd better hurry," Calvin said.

I picked up my pace. I still had no idea what would happen when we actually got to the shop, but somebody had to do something.

When we turned the corner into the alley, the sky grew darker, as if the storm clouds overhead were leaning in for a better view. I nearly tripped over a small figure huddled against the wall near an overflowing garbage can. It was the little boy from the day before, the one who'd been chasing Gomo.

"Why won't you talk to me?" the boy blubbered, cradling the garden gnome to his chest. Except Gomo no longer had animated features and a belly like a balloon. He was an ordinary garden statue made of stone, his eyes and mouth both drawn on with paint. "Gomo, I didn't mean to make you fly. Please talk to me."

I gave Calvin a look that said, Yikes, let's move on. We eased past the boy and approached The Shop of Last Resort. The doorway stood open, but I didn't hear any chattering or shouting like the day before. I stepped inside and gasped. Like all of Main Street, the shop looked completely empty.

Not only that, it was like a miniature tornado had swept through, leaving a trail of debris and broken shelves in its wake.

"Everything's gone," Calvin said, walking past me to stand in the center of the shop.

He was right. Every shelf in the small room was bare, as was the Odds & Ends bin. Not a single broken hairbrush or bent TV antenna. Pieces of the crystal chandelier lay shattered on the pink carpet, along with a tangle of twisted train tracks.

A low growling noise erupted from behind a fallen shelf.

"What was that?" Calvin said, returning to where I was standing over by the counter. "It sounded like . . ."

He didn't have time to finish, because the rumbling growl came again, and we both saw a long orange-and-black tail emerge from behind the fallen shelving, swishing back and forth in the air.

"Is that . . ." Calvin gulped. "Mr. Winkles?"

"I guess," I said, but the truth was the tail looked way too big to belong to Mr. Winkles. It was more like something you'd find attached to a full-grown tiger.

"Maybe we should come back later," Calvin suggested, easing toward the door, but just then the bead curtain tinkled and a beautiful woman greeted us with a smile.

"Now there you are, puddin' pies. I'm afraid I haven't got much on offer at the moment." I looked at Calvin, and I could tell we were thinking the exact same thing. This woman most definitely had to be Mag, but she couldn't be. Her white-blond hair hung in bouncy waves that draped down past her curvy waist. She looked about Mom's age, maybe younger, with bright eyes, smooth skin, and not one tiny hint of wrinkles. "Actually, I was just packing up." She hefted a small box onto the furry countertop. I recognized a few of the items from the Restricted Section inside.

"Packing up?" Calvin said, squeezing so close to me our arms touched.

"That's right. I never like to overstay my welcome," she said in her perky southern drawl. "Besides, I'm plum out of merchandise. Now." She leaned down close, plumping her lips in Calvin's direction. "Is there something I can do for you, cutie? You look like you came here on a mission."

Calvin opened his mouth, then shut it again. Don't get me wrong. Calvin was my best friend ever, and he definitely had his own special superpowers, but standing up to witchy vampire ladies wasn't exactly one of them.

I cleared my throat. Mag turned her twinkly eyes on me,

and I pulled off my hat. I could tell from her expression that she got the picture.

"Oh, hon, is that what you're worried about? A few white hairs?" She ran a finger through her own luxurious curls. "It'll fade in a day or two. Along with any other . . . lingering side effects. Don't you worry one tiny bit. Before you know it, you'll be good as new!" She continued to pack up the small box, as if turning people's hair gray with her magic was nothing to get upset about.

I sputtered, trying to think of a reply, when my gaze drifted to the items she was packing. I saw a cracked pipe filled with old tobacco leaves, labeled, "For honesty." A chipped perfume bottle with a tag that read, "For beauty." She lifted up the last item and examined it in the dim light spilling in from the street. It was the top half of a candlestick with dried trails of wax dripping down the side. The label said, "For warding."

"What does that one do?" I said. Calvin stared at me in disbelief. "I'm . . . just asking."

"Yeah, right," Calvin said, a sudden flash of anger crossing his face. "I'll be outside. Are you coming?"

I hesitated. Mag was leaving. We'd gotten what we came for, without even trying. I knew how wrong the love spells had been. But this . . . maybe it would be different.

"I'll be there in a second."

Calvin's eye feelings shot arrows at my already-exhausted heart. I watched him turn and walk away.

"Poor thing," Mag clucked, sucking her tongue against her perfect white teeth. "Don't think that love spell I gave him worked out the way he wanted." She gave me a funny look, an amused smile playing on her lips, then handed me the broken candlestick. "Now, I don't usually give this out to just anyone," Mag confided, fluttering her long, thick eye-lashes. "There's a whole lot of magic trapped in the wax." She tapped it with her nail and a curl of white wax crumbled to the fuzzy countertop.

"'Warding' means protection against evil. All you have to do is carve the source of your troubles right here, in the wax, and abracadabra, your woes will disappear. More or less." She gave a dramatic flourish with her totally non-veiny hands, and then went right back to packing. Not that she had much left, just that one tiny box. Behind me, I could hear the low growls of Mr. Winkles start up again, like an engine, and they seemed to be inching closer.

"And I can write anything? Even . . . a name?" The words tingled on my lips. I shouldn't. I couldn't. But why not? This was all *his* fault.

"That's right, honey bunch! Easy as pie." With the box packed, she pulled on a leopard-print poncho and waved toward the shelves. "Time to go, Winkie Poo! Say goodbye to your new friend."

I stepped back as a pair of huge yellow eyes appeared from behind the fallen shelves. No way they belonged to the puff ball that was Mr. Winkles, except . . . a claw emerged, bearing the same orange-and-black-striped fur. But it was enormous, nearly the size of my face.

"Um . . . I should probably go find Calvin," I said, backing into the door frame. "So you're really leaving town?" I said, reminded again of our mission. It had all been so easy. "And everyone will go back to normal?"

Mag's plump pink lips lifted into a friendly smile. "Like I said, we never like to overstay our welcome. Besides," she said, taking out a compact and powdering her perfectly perky nose, "we got what we wanted, didn't we, Mr. Winkie Pants?"

The fallen shelf tipped forward as a massive form emerged from the wreckage. I didn't stick around to see Mag's new-and-improved pet. I rushed out the door, stumbling straight into Calvin. "Time to go," I said, grabbing his sleeve and dragging him up the alley, down the street, and all the way back to our bikes.

When I finally paused for a breath, I saw his eyes go directly to the candlestick still gripped in my hand. "You're not seriously going to use that?"

"No, I just . . ." I knew he wouldn't understand. I wasn't even sure I did, but if there was any chance to put things right, even a tiny one, I had to try. Didn't I? I knew what JUNIEPIE28 would say. That I couldn't control other people's lives. But Mom and Dad weren't other people! And I was tired of everyone telling me that it was complicated and there was nothing I could do.

I looked down at the candlestick and then back up at Calvin. "I'm not like you," I said. "I have to try."

"What's that supposed to mean?"

I could see the hurt on Calvin's face, but I kept going. This wasn't about him. "I can't just sit back and do nothing, that's all."

"Like me?"

Calvin's words opened up the hollow again in my stomach, but I didn't back down. I wasn't trying to be mean. "No, that's not what I said."

"But that's what you're thinking, right?" He grabbed his handlebars and dragged his bike away from me. "Poor Calvin didn't try hard enough, and now he only sees his dad at Christmas."

"I didn't say that. Wait!"

Calvin climbed on his bike, looking everywhere but at my face. "Whatever. If you think I'm such a failure, why do you even hang out with me?" He punched down the pedals, wobbling over the cobbled street. He'd only gone a few feet when he turned back. "Have fun not helping out at the ball."

What was that supposed to mean?

"Calvin, come back!" I called, but it was too late. I watched him ride away, nearly falling on the uneven stones, but eventually bumping his way to the asphalt and speeding off.

Great.

I had one more chance to get Mom and Dad back together, but I'd lost my best friend in the process. Seriously, life. Why do you have to stink so much all the time?

With Calvin gone, I spent a few more minutes watching all the happy couples in The Friendly Bean. If Gavin had never come along, that would still be Mom and Dad. In a normal, not-forgetting-I-exist kind of way. I took a deep breath and dug my pocketknife from my backpack.

This was it.

Last chance.

I closed my eyes and pictured what it would be like if Gavin moved away. Or, better yet, if he'd never even existed. Mom and Dad dancing at the Bigfoot Ball, Dad's hair all clean and smoothed back, Mom in her silky green dress with the tiny beads that sparkled like scales. The three of us sitting around a huge cake for my thirteenth birthday, bigfoot shaped of course, blowing out the candles and laughing. Maybe they'd win the lotto—not a lot, just enough for Mom to open a little art studio downtown, like she'd always wanted.

Everything would be perfect. The way it should be.

I unfolded the blade of my pocketknife and dug the tip into the wax. It cut through easily as I made the curve of the *G*, the slant of the *A*. Slivers of wax dropped onto my sneakers with each letter: *V*, *I*, and finally the jagged, razor-edged *N*.

When I was finished, I held the candle out at arm's length and examined my work. A cloud of dread draped itself around my shoulders, all heavy and wet with rain. Whatever. I shook it off and shoved the candle into the bottom of my backpack.

This would work.

This time would be different.

It had to be.

I wheeled my bike to the point where the cobbles turned to a black sheet of asphalt. I drew in a long breath, trying to slow my racing heart. Only one thing left to do now. I had to go back home and see if anything had happened.

Trees rushed past as I zoomed down the road, my nostrils filling with the scent of cows, sap, and freshly mown grass. I took the long way around, winding through Calvin's neighborhood with its fancy houses and neatly trimmed lawns. No sign of his bike leaning against the garage where he normally left it.

I pedaled on without slowing, telling myself I didn't care about Calvin. If he wanted to be mad at me, that was his problem, not mine. I took the next right out of the neighborhood and back onto the main road. A swaying wheat field flitted past on my left, overgrown trees on my right, their thin, drooping branches tangled up in clumps of weeds and vines.

I passed the back entrance to Tanglewood Village, the saggy chain-link fence, the line of green dumpsters crawling with raccoons and sun-baked bags of trash. My feet punched the pedals, racing onward. Part of me wanted to give the magic time to work. The other part? Okay, so maybe I was a little freaked. The annoying cloud was back again, pressing me down into my seat, wobbling on my shoulders and drenching me with teardrops of hot, sticky rain.

I'd wished that someone would go away, that they'd never existed. I'd carved his name into the candle and now . . . would he have to leave Mom alone? Would it be like he'd never been born? Who was I to decide what happened to a total stranger?

A wave of acid pushed its way up my throat, but I swallowed it back down again. No, this was different. It was Gavin. He'd tried to steal Mom away. He deserved whatever he got. Didn't he?

I rounded the final corner and pulled to a stop at the entrance to the trailer park. I watched a crow pecking bits of paint from the sign that read TANGLEWOOD VILLAGE.

Deep breaths. You can do this.

I closed my eyes and pictured the future I wanted, going back through all the images I'd imagined when I was standing outside The Friendly Bean. Positive thinking. This would work.

Letting out my breath, I opened my eyes and pedaled for home.

I expected to find Dad outside working on Honey Pie, or maybe patching up the roof. The yard was empty apart from the dancing wind chimes and the clink, clink, clink of Dad's beer bottle whirligig. I thought briefly of Gomo, all frozen and stony eyed, but pushed the image from my mind. I propped my bike against the side of the trailer and eased open the door.

"Dad? Are you here?"

CHAPTER 16

OTHER MOTHER

The trailer was dark apart from the sunlight peeking in through the blinds and the glow from the TV set. "Is anyone here?" The living room smelled like dirty laundry, stale beer, and cigarette smoke. I moved toward the sickly halo cast by the TV, and there was Dad, lounging in his recliner, sitting alone in the dark in the middle of the afternoon.

"There you are, baby," he said, turning to me with a smile, his eyes all shiny from drinking. He had the same shaggy hair and unshaved face, but he looked different somehow. I followed a trail of orange crumbs down his shirt.

"Wanna watch *Motorcycle Rehab*? They got a real good one on today. A Harley-Davidson that they're tricking out with a sound system and mini fridge. Should be sweet."

"No, thanks," I said, the inside of my mouth numb. I took a seat on the edge of the coffee table and studied Dad more closely. He looked so different. Like he hadn't slept in weeks. He picked up a lit cigarette from an ashtray and brought it to his lips.

"You never smoke in the house," I said, my voice coming out quieter than usual. My whole body felt small in the presence of this new, strange Dad.

He peeled the cigarette from his lips and stubbed it out in the ashtray. "Thought you were gone," he said, giving my shoulder a squeeze and reaching over to turn on a fan. "What you get up to today, baby? Anything fun?"

"No, I . . . Why are you inside? Don't you have any jobs today?"

"Jobs? Aw, man, not you too. Your mom won't shut up about me getting a real job. Like she don't work enough hours for the both of us?"

I froze, not liking the edge that crept into his voice at the mention of Mom. What was happening? This was all so . . . wrong. "Where is Mom anyway?"

Dad took another swig of beer and wiped his mouth. "Where you think she is? At work, like always. Couldn't stand to spend an afternoon with me, so she had to go work another double shift."

"Double shift?"

"Yeah, baby. She's down at the Gas 'n' Go, where else?" He leaned back in his chair, his head pressing into the grease-stained cushion. "Sometimes I think she can't even stand to look at me."

"But, Dad," I said, putting a hand on the knee of his sweatpants. "She loves you. Aren't you two going to the ball tonight?"

Dad snorted, spit flying from his mouth and landing on the coffee table. "You gotta be kidding me! Not like I didn't ask her though. But you know your mom. She's all about making money. And what's she planning to spend it on anyway? It's not like she ever does anything anymore besides work."

Dad's eyes trailed off, focusing on the TV, and he sank back farther into the folds of his recliner.

Shaken and at a loss for words, I walked straight back out the door and closed it softly behind me. This wasn't my dad. It couldn't be. And what did he mean about Mom?

She'd always hated working at the Gas 'n' Go. She only picked up a few shifts here and there for extra money. I tried to take a deep breath, to calm my nerves, but my heart had lodged itself inside my throat.

I had to find Mom. This wasn't at all how I'd imagined it. How could getting rid of Gavin turn Dad into that?

Once I'd broken the last spell, some of my energy had returned, but now my legs were bricks of hardened Play-Doh. I lifted one leg over my bike with a grunt and settled my aching butt into the seat.

"You can do this," I said aloud, sending my dead muscles some positive vibes. I had to do this. I turned the handlebars and pedaled over the grass. Each rotation was like wading through quicksand, but I pushed onward, sweat dribbling down my forehead and the back of my neck. I left Tanglewood Village behind, wheezing with the effort, and was soon on my way to Route 3.

The Gas 'n' Go was on the outskirts of town, not far from Mom's pond and Dino Land. When I reached Route 3, i.e., the highway that cut through town, I pulled onto the shoulder, narrowly avoiding a collision with a semitruck. Usually, I could cut across the two-lane road in no time, but today it was like swimming through wet concrete. The bright red semi blasted me with its horn and barreled past. I closed my eyes against the spray of smoke and sharp rocks that rose up in its wake.

My breath grew thinner as I forced my legs to keep moving up and down on the pedals, bringing me closer and closer to Mom. After what felt like hours, but was really only a few minutes, I passed the turnoff for Dino Land and the pond and kept on going till I came to a dirty white pavilion with six old-fashioned gas pumps. I slumped to a stop at the edge of the parking lot, and here's what I saw: a bunch of shabby pickups and shiny semis; an ice machine that was always grinding and grumbling, sending up curls of white smoke; truckers cussing and spitting on the sidewalk; a smashed hot dog covered in flies; a shop with glass windows covered in ads and finger smudges.

I wheeled my bike across the parking lot, dragging air into my shriveled lungs. I leaned it up against the ice machine and pressed my face to the smudgy glass.

There was Mom.

She wore a grubby orange-and-green uniform with a long grease stain down the front. Usually, she'd bring her special name tag any time she had to work, the one that she and I had decorated together. We'd used about a million sequins and colored duct tape, and Dad had shown me how to twist the duct tape into flowers with delicate leaves. Mom said the name tag helped her get through the day, because it reminded her of home. Today she wore a cold, plastic tag with KATHERINE typed out in big block letters.

Katherine? Mom always went by Kat. She said Katherine was a name for an accountant or a banker, something boring like that. Kat was the name of a true artist.

I watched Mom hand some trucker lady her change, her expression empty, blank. Usually, Mom was all friendly words and quiet smiles. Whenever customers left, she'd whip out her sketchbook, and her eyes would go all dreamy and she'd turn the crusty slushy machine or the dirty ATM into something beautiful. She'd always show me her sketches when she got home from work, and I'd gape, amazed that she could make stuff that was so ugly look so unique and interesting.

The door jangled as trucker lady came outside, leaving the shop empty. Except for Mom. I waited for Mom to take out her sketchbook and start drawing, but she didn't. Instead, she sat on a stool behind the register, frown lines weighing down her face, just staring out the opposite window. And it wasn't the stare of an artist, searching for sparks of true beauty;

it was a vacant, glassy-eyed stare. Like Mom was looking, but not seeing anything at all. And her hair was different too. It wasn't pale pink anymore, like cotton candy, but a boring, dingy blond.

The bell over the door clanged as I stepped inside.

"June?" Mom said, confusion in her glassy eyes. "What are you doing here?" A flicker of a smile appeared on Mom's face, but it might as well have been a ghost. It faded almost instantly. She looked tired. Exhausted actually. She looked the way I felt.

I stood there by the counter, not knowing what to do with my hands. Inside, my brain was sending up a panic signal, but I had to stay calm. This could still all work out. I stared at the grease stain on Mom's shirt, avoiding her vacant eyes. "I wanted to see you. How are you feeling?"

"Fine, hon. Just fine," Mom said. Once again, that ghost of a smile. Her eyes trailed off to a roach motel partially hidden under the register. She studied it for long seconds, before blinking, as if she'd just remembered I was there. "How are you? Do anything fun today?" Her voice was so sad, like someone had drained out any hint of happiness.

"I'm . . . fine. But I'm worried about you. Dad said you're working all the time."

A darkness passed behind Mom's eyes, but then it was gone, just like her ghost of a smile. "Why don't you come sit down for a while," Mom said in her heavy, wooden voice. "Let's talk." I followed Mom behind the counter. I had always wondered what it looked like back there, especially when I was younger. It was . . . less awesome than I'd expected. Candy wrappers and empty soda cans littered the floor next to two overflowing trash bins. Flies buzzed around Mom's ankles, but it was like she hardly noticed them. And she wasn't wearing her usual army boots either, the ones with rainbow beads woven into the laces, but a pair of white orthopedic shoes. A fly settled in between the Velcro straps, rubbing its spindly black legs.

"Sit over here," Mom said. She cleared off two dusty cardboard boxes, and we each took a seat. "Now, tell me what's the matter. Is it your dad? Is he smoking in the house again?"

The words cut into me. Not just because she was right, he had been smoking, but because something had clearly gone horribly wrong. Getting rid of Gavin was supposed to put Mom and Dad back to normal, not change them into totally different people. People who didn't even like each other.

I watched the dark circles under Mom's eyes, her drooping shoulders, the deep lines at the sides of her mouth, trying to figure out how to begin. "Mom?"

"Yeah, sweetie?" she said, looking at the overflowing trash bin and not at me. "What is it?"

"Do you still have your sketchbook?" I searched the grimy shelves under the counter, packed full of receipt paper and more roach motels.

Mom laughed. A single sharp burst that ended with her clearing her throat. "Hon, where'd that come from? What would I need with a sketchbook? You know I can't draw anything but stick figures." She gave me a strange look, like she was trying to work out what was going on inside my head. "Besides, I don't have time for that. Carl finally gave me those extra shifts I wanted, did I tell you? Now I'll be making almost double the money. This time next year we can finally get out of that dump of a trailer and buy a real house."

"A *real* house?" I said, each word coming out slowly, like pulling a tooth. "But we have a real house. I love our trailer. It's home."

Mom finally swatted at one of the flies on her shoe.

"You know what? Sometimes you're just like your dad." She puckered up her lips for a second, as if being like Dad was the worst thing in the world, then her lips settled back into a thin, pale line.

"But you love to draw. Remember? What about art school? Don't you ever miss it?"

Mom laughed again. "Where are you getting all this, June? From your dad? I never liked to draw. Waste of time. One of us actually has to work unless we want to get kicked out on the street." The anger built up in Mom's voice, then drained away again.

She looked at me, apology written in her ragged features. "I guess there was that one summer," she said, eyes drifting toward the window, distant. "I was eight or nine, and my dad tried to send me to some art camp in the woods. I said no. It was all this hippie-dippie, finding-beauty-in-nature crap. Not for me at all." Her eyes shifted to the moldy ceiling tiles, remembering. "I mean, if any of my friends had been going it might have been different. There was this one boy." For a moment, Mom's lips lifted into an actual smile. "Gavin. I had the biggest crush on him, and he was really into art. He even drew me a picture once of our wedding day. Now, if he'd been going . . ."

"Wait, his name was Gavin?" Heart. Escaping. Chest. Cavity. "And he loved art?"

"Oh yeah. We were best friends. He had this amazing way of turning the most boring stuff into something beautiful." Her eyes took on their familiar dreamy quality, but they were still tinged with sadness. "I'd follow him around his backyard, which was littered with trash and old car parts, but he'd paint these pictures where everything looked all pretty and full of wonder. It was . . . I don't know . . . almost like magic."

"So why didn't you go to art camp with Gavin?"

"Oh." Mom swatted another fly and the spell was broken. "He moved away right before. I thought we'd keep in touch." She sighed, the fluorescent lights casting hard shadows down her cheeks. "But I never heard from him again."

"That's awful," I said. The room around me had started to spin. The harsh light inside was growing dim, and it felt like I was being pulled down a dark tunnel. This couldn't be happening. Gavin was . . . terrible. He was the reason Mom and Dad were breaking up. The reason my life was turning upside down.

Could he also be the reason Mom was Mom? The reason she'd become an artist and learned to see the world in a strange and beautiful way?

My heart sank deep into my chest, barely even remembering to beat. But what about Dad? Why was he so different?

Smoking in the house? Watching TV all day like he didn't care about anything, even Honey Pie? It didn't make sense . . . except, maybe it did.

Mom wasn't Mom because she hadn't gone to that art camp with Gavin. What if Dad wasn't Dad because he'd never fallen in love with Mom? At least not the real Mom.

"But you could still learn," I said, grasping for anything that could get my failure of a plan back on track. "About art. If you gave it a chance, I know you'd start to love it."

"What?" Mom nearly choked, turning to me with disbelieving eyes. "Are you sure you're okay?" She felt my forehead, checking for fever. "Honey, I can't draw, remember? Besides, Gavin was the one who cared about art."

The tunnel that was the Gas 'n' Go closed in around me. "Come on. Maybe we could draw something right now," I said, my voice shaking with desperation. If I could remind Mom how much she loved art, maybe, somehow, she'd be herself again and this would all—

The bell over the door jangled, and two truckers came in asking for cigarettes. Mom got to her feet with a grunt. "That'll be fifteen eighty-five," Mom said, all traces of life drained from her voice. She gave them their change, and then more customers came in. A girl in a spaghetti strap tank and no shoes, a guy swirling a wad of chewing tobacco around in his mouth.

"Sorry, hon, better get back to work," Mom said, her dead eyes trailing the customers, not even bothering to look my way.

"But . . ." I started to argue, but I could see it was no use. I watched as the flies settled deeper into the grooves of Mom's shoes, and then I picked up my backpack and dragged myself out the door.

Total. Absolute. Disaster.

With barely enough energy to walk, I wheeled my bike around to the back of the gas station and slumped down on a stack of newspapers. The clouds churned overhead as I pulled the candlestick from my backpack. I held it up, arm throbbing from the effort, and studied the shaky letters I'd cut in the wax.

"GAVIN."

This had all started with him. But maybe not in the way I'd first imagined. My heart sank even deeper in my chest, and then it slipped out through my rib cage and flopped down onto the dirty pavement. A fly buzzed past my ear and alighted on one of the bloody, sputtering ventricles.

Swallowing down a sob, I dug around in my backpack

until my fingers closed around a small box of matches. I lit the bottom of the candle first, until the wax started dripping, and then I pressed the melty end firmly into the pavement, right next to my oozing, fly-encrusted heart. Next, I lit the wick and watched my last hope of stopping the divorce slowly burn away before my eyes.

CHAPTER 17

I GUESS THIS IS GOODBYE

Melting the candle took longer than I expected.
Images from before, of Mom and Dad dancing and happy at the Bigfoot Ball, played on repeat in my head. It was all dropping away from me. Like I really was trapped in a tunnel, or a black hole, and everything I'd ever known was disintegrating.

I watched the flickering flame, imagining my vision board going up in smoke too, the poster board and all the happy pictures curling and crumbling into ash. The world around me was spinning again, flies buzzing, heart burbling out its last few drops of blood. I had to make it stop.

I took out the laptop and pressed the power button.

While I waited for the screen to load, for the candle to burn down, I took off my bigfoot hat and ran a hand through my sweaty hair. I held a few strands in front of me, examining them. I didn't just have a white streak anymore. All of it, every chunk I could see, had turned a stark, snowy white.

Great.

I tied my hair in a knot at the top of my head and pulled the hat over my ears. The desktop background filled in pixel by pixel. I logged on to the Gas 'n' Go Wi-Fi and opened up Hi-hi! A new chat box appeared from JUNIEPIE15.

JUNIEPIE15: Hello! Are you there?

BIGFOOT_GRL: I'm here. How are you?

Talking to Past Me was weirdly comforting. I waited for her to answer, surprised to find that the world had already stopped spinning around me, for the most part. Burning the candle was the right thing to do. Now I just had to hope it worked.

JUNIEPIE15: I'm super great! Calvin and I get to help out at the Bigfoot Ball tonight! We're serving finger sandwiches. Gross! But it will still be fun because Calvin's there.

BIGFOOT_GRL: You know finger sandwiches aren't made from real fingers, right?

JUNIEPIE15: Duh! Of course I know that!

She so totally didn't.

JUNIEPIE15: Hey, I've been meaning to ask you, what's Calvin doing now? Is he still funny and cute and stuff?

BIGFOOT_GRL: Cute?

JUNIEPIE15: Not like that! Ew! I just mean . . . we're still best friends, right?

Heart. Sinking. Ventricles. Oozing.

For some reason, I thought back to Dad smoking in his armchair, all greasy and covered in crumbs. Mom staring glassy-eyed at the gas station window, not even noticing the flies burrowing into her shoes. All that had happened because I'd wished one of Mom's friends away.

And now, because of me, Calvin and I weren't speaking.

JUNIEPIE15: Hello? Did you hear me?

BIGFOOT_GRL: Yeah, sorry. We're . . . kind of fighting right now.

JUNIEPIE15: WHAT!!! You and Calvin! No way! You have to make up with him right now!

BIGFOOT_GRL: It's . . . sigh . . . complicated.

JUNIEPIE15: No, it's not! Calvin is my best friend, and you can't change that! Go say you're sorry. Right now. That's an order!

BIGFOOT_GRL: Hey, how do you know it's my fault?

JUNIEPIE15: Well, isn't it?

Double sigh.

The annoying thing was, she was right. I watched the candlelight flicker as a rainy mist settled over the parking lot. I held my hand over the flame, so it wouldn't snuff out.

BIGFOOT_GRL: Fine, I'll apologize.

JUNIEPIE15: You'd better!

BIGFOOT_GRL: I am!

JUNIEPIE15: Good!

Wow, Past Me was a total bossy pants. But the truth was, I would miss her.

BIGFOOT_GRL: Hey, I probably won't be talking to you again for a while.

JUNIEPIE15: I know.

BIGFOOT_GRL: You do?

JUNIEPIE15: Yeah, just a feeling.

BIGFOOT_GRL: But I'm glad I got to meet you. And thanks.

JUNIEPIE15: For what?

BIGFOOT_GRL: For helping me do the right thing.

JUNIEPIE15: No problemo.

BIGFOOT_GRL: Well, I guess this is goodbye.

JUNIEPIE15: Wait, one more thing.

BIGFOOT_GRL: Yeah?

JUNIEPIE15: Are you sure you don't think Calvin's cute? Just a little?

BIGFOOT_GRL: Hey! Enough with the cute! I have to go.

JUNIEPIE15: Whatever. Bye, Future Me.

BIGFOOT_GRL: Bye. ☺

I thought about giving her some advice, like JUNIEPIE28 had given me, but the chat box had already disappeared. Besides, knowing me, she wouldn't listen.

I opened a new chat window with Calvin.

BIGFOOT_GRL: Hey. I'm sorry about today. Really sorry. Still friends?

Mom and Dad were getting a divorce. It was happening, and there was nothing I could do to stop it. JUNIEPIE28 had been right. There were some things in life you couldn't control. But this . . . my friendship with Calvin . . .

My heart, magically back in my chest, seized up at the sight of three blinking dots below my last message. Calvin was typing.

CALTHEDESTROYER: Still friends. ☺ I'm sorry too.
CALTHEDESTROYER: So, how did it all work out?

I thought about lying and saying that I'd decided not to use the magic, but this was Calvin. He deserved to hear the truth.

BIGFOOT_GRL: I think absolutely terrible about sums it up.

CALTHEDESTROYER: Oh, sorry. Hey, my hair's almost back to normal. I think Mag was telling the truth.

BIGFOOT_GRL: That's good to hear.

I didn't tell him about my new granny-chic hairdo. Hopefully it would fade before he saw me again.

CALTHEDESTROYER: So, do you have any more secret missions? I'm not judging, really. I know you're just trying to help. I shouldn't have been so mean about it before. I think I was just . . . I don't know, feeling like maybe you were right. Maybe I didn't try hard enough to stop my parents' divorce.

BIGFOOT_GRL: First of all, I was so not right. You couldn't have done anything to change it. I know that now. It wasn't up to you.

Wow, I was really starting to sound like JUNIEPIE28. Awesome. That was sarcasm, by the way, in case you didn't notice.

BIGFOOT_GRL: Second, I am so completely over secret missions. And lists, and elaborate plans of all kinds.

CALTHEDESTROYER: Seriously?

I considered.

BIGFOOT_GRL: Well, COMPLETELY might be a bit of an overstatement . . .

CALTHEDESTROYER: Hahaha. That's what I thought.

Another chat box popped up with a ping.

BIGFOOT_GRL: Hey, Cal, I have to go. But we're all good now, right?

CALTHEDESTROYER: Definitely.

BIGFOOT_GRL: Cool. Talk soon.

CALTHEDESTROYER: June?

BIGFOOT_GRL: Yeah?

CALTHEDESTROYER: About that letter. You're not going to read it, right? You'll just throw it away?

With everything going on, it took me a minute to remember what letter Calvin was talking about.

BIGFOOT_GRL: Sure. But what's the big deal? What'd you write in there anyway?

CALTHEDESTROYER: Nothing! Like I said, it was totally embarrassing, and I just don't want to make things weird between us.

BIGFOOT_GRL: Weird how?

CALTHEDESTROYER: Never mind. Just don't read it. Pinky swear?

BIGFOOT_GRL: Okay, pinky swear.

BIGFOOT_GRL: Bye, Cal.

CALTHEDESTROYER: Bye.

I clicked over to the new chat box and saw a message from JUNIEPIE28. My eyes drifted over to the candlestick. Only an inch left before it would completely burn down into a pool of bubbling wax.

JUNIEPIE28: So, I guess this is it, huh, kid? Lesson learned and all that?

BIGFOOT_GRL: I guess.

JUNIEPIE28: Sorry my advice was so totally useless. What can I say? I tried my best.

BIGFOOT_GRL: No, you helped. Really. Like you said, I think I just had to go through it myself. The way you did.

JUNIEPIE28: Yeah, but still. I was hoping to stop your heart from spilling out on the pavement. Looks like I failed on that count.

BIGFOOT_GRL: Yeah, but it'll heal.

JUNIEPIE28: Hey, Diaper Baby, maybe you're smarter than I thought.

BIGFOOT_GRL: Rude! I am not a Diaper Baby!

JUNIEPIE28: Kidding, geez!

BIGFOOT_GRL: So . . . what now?

JUNIEPIE28: For me? Dancing, studying, a big scary chem test.

BIGFOOT_GRL: No, for me.

JUNIEPIE28: Self-centered much? Okay, okay, joking. Now you live your life. That's it. It won't be perfect. There's no secret key to unlock the future you've always dreamed of, where everything is exactly like you imagined. But I guess you know that now.

BIGFOOT_GRL: Big-time.

JUNIEPIE28: You'll go back home and talk to Mom and Dad. They still love you, you know? Like so much, it's embarrassing. And you'll figure out something that works for everyone, and that'll be that.

BIGFOOT_GRL: And the magic?

JUNIEPIE28: Oh, you mean your new fabulous hairdo? That'll fade in a few days. Of course, there is one kind of sad thing.

BIGFOOT_GRL: What?

I watched the last of the candlestick's walls collapse, spilling a wave of clear wax onto the cement. I kept my hand in place, waiting for the flame to die down.

JUNIEPIE28: The laptop. You have to get rid of it. Unless you like the whole I'm-a-granny-at-twelve look.

BIGFOOT_GRL: Yeah, not so much. Besides, I kind of figured.

JUNIEPIE28: So I guess we won't be talking again.

BIGFOOT_GRL: Guess not.

BIGFOOT_GRL: Good luck with your chem test.

JUNIEPIE28: Thanks! Good luck with, you know, everything.

BIGFOOT_GRL: Thanks. ☺

JUNIEPIE28: Oh, and can I give you one last piece of advice?

BIGFOOT_GRL: Like I could stop you.

JUNIEPIE28: True. Read the letter. The one Calvin sent.

BIGFOOT_GRL: But he said not to.

JUNIEPIE28: Just trust me on this one.

BIGFOOT_GRL: Okay, if you say so.

JUNIEPIE28: I say so. Bye, Diaper Baby. Go have a great life.

BIGFOOT_GRL: You too!

With that, the flame burned out, and JUNIEPIE28's chat box disappeared. I let out a long breath, noticing how the world had stopped spinning completely. There was even a thin sliver of sun peeking through the clouds. I closed the laptop with a click. Already, my energy was returning, my muscles still stiff but working more or less like normal.

I picked up the heavy laptop and let it teeter on the edge of the dumpster. Dad might not understand why I'd thrown away his gift, but I didn't have much of a choice. The laptop was full of magic, and magic was so not me. At least not anymore. I tipped the laptop forward, and then let go, only cringing a little as it hit the bottom of the dumpster with a reverberating crack.

After that, I pulled my backpack over my shoulders, now much lighter without the weight of the laptop, and headed back around to the front. I didn't know what to expect when I looked inside, but instead of Mom standing behind the counter, it was Mom's boss, Carl. I watched him for a moment as he aimed and tried to swat a fly, before climbing on my bike.

My legs surged with energy as I pedaled down the highway, relishing the feel of the cool mist on my face. My first thought was to head for home, but then the sign for Dino Land came into view, and I punched the brakes, veering off down the gravel drive.

I left my bike by the fence and walked the rest of the way to the pond. Even though I knew the spell should be reversed, my heart still clenched at the thought of seeing Mom.

The pond looked just the way I'd left it—dragonflies buzzing, birds chattering, the tall grass tickling my calves. And there, parked in a tangle of weeds and vines, sat the silver submarine. I came around to the front of the RV to find Mom's easel and a half-finished canvas. Unlike her usual nature scenes, this one was a rough sketch of me when I was little, splashing in the water, probably at Sardis Lake. I looked down and there, in a puddle of mud right where I'd left it, was the creepy mood painting. Except now the sunflowers weren't dead and rotting. They were gone. Washed away by all the rain and mud.

I was about to go knock on the door of the submarine when a branch cracked on the other side of the pond. A huge shadow disappeared into the branches, moving with lithe, animal-like grace. Gram's face swam into my head, and I remembered the strange eyes I had glimpsed the other day, watching me from the forest. Could this be it? Could I finally prove all of Gram's theories about bigfoot right once and for all?

Palms tingling, I moved quietly around the rim of the pond and stepped through an archway of branches. The archway led to a narrow path that twisted back, deep into the forest. The smell of pine and wet bark filled my nostrils, but that wasn't all.

Another branch cracked up ahead. That tingling deep in my gut pulled me forward, and suddenly I was running.

Vines slapping my face, damp grass tracing patterns on my ankles. I stopped at the edge of a small clearing, lit by a slant of sunlight.

In the middle of the clearing, hand held over her eyes to block out the sun, stood a girl. She was facing away from me, but I could tell she was about my age. A sheet of gold-white hair trailed behind her, lifting gently on the wind. The strands sparkled in the bright rays, almost like her hair was made of starlight, and standing by her side, haunches flexed, stood a tiger.

There was nothing left of the wrinkly, pudgy soccer ball that had been Mr. Winkles. Now he was a full-grown tiger, bigger than any I'd ever seen, his sinewy back reaching up past the girl's shoulders. She laid a hand on his glistening orange-and-black coat, whispering something in his ear, and then the girl and the tiger disappeared deeper into the forest.

The thought crossed my mind that I should follow, but I stayed put. I didn't know if I would ever see Mag and Mr. Winkles again, but I knew that our story was finished. At least for now.

I made my way slowly back to the pond. Mom's pond. I was walking toward the door to the submarine when it swung open.

Gavin stepped out, a look of mild surprise on his face. The really weird part was, I was actually happy to see him.

"Oh, hey. I didn't expect to see you here. This is . . . um . . . kind of awkward," he said, rubbing the brownish-blond hair of his goatee. "Sorry, that was a weird thing to say. Hi, we haven't really met. I'm Gavin." He came down the steps and held out his hand. He had a tangle of braided leather bracelets on his wrist and a tattoo of a paintbrush.

Gavin. He was the reason for all my failed missions. The reason Mom had missed my birthday. The reason she was leaving Dad, and me, for a fancy new life in New York. Then again, he was also the reason Mom was Mom, and Dad was Dad.

I told myself I should shake his hand, or say hello, or at least not stand there like I had Play-Doh for brains.

Yeah, I didn't. I might have learned my lesson, but that didn't mean I was ready to make friends.

"No worries." He stuffed his hands into the pockets of his cargo shorts and made one of those wow-this-is-super-awkward emoji faces. "I wouldn't want to shake my hand either. I . . . No, I probably shouldn't say anything, but just so you know . . . I mean, your mom and I never meant for anything to happen. It just sort of . . . happened." He cupped his hands over his face, groaning. "Sorry, worst conversation ever, right? You maybe don't know this, but your mom and I have been friends for a long time. Since we were like five. She grew up in the house across the street from me."

I stared at Gavin, watching his cheeks turn redder by the second.

"And I want you to know, I'm not taking your mom away from you. That's the last thing I want, promise. It's . . . man, I'm really bad at this. It's just, you know—"

"Don't say complicated," I cut in, because I'd heard it way too many times before. Even if it was true.

"I was . . . totally going to say complicated. Sorry. I must sound like a bad after-school special."

"What does that even mean?"

"Oh, um, never mind. These terrible TV movies from the nineties. I guess you weren't even born then, huh?"

"Not exactly."

He shook his head, then scratched his goatee for a while, then went back to shaking his head. Pathetic.

"So, is my mom here?" I said, breaking the silence.

"Oh, no. She left. Actually, I think she went looking for you. Something about needing to talk about the way she'd left things last night."

"Cool," I said. To my surprise, I found that I was almost smiling at how truly pitiful this guy looked. "You could have started with that, you know?"

"Right. That might have been better. Sorry."

I shook my head and climbed on my bike.

"Wait, June, hang on."

"Yeah?" I turned back and looked at Gavin. Was this really the guy I'd been so mad at that I'd wished him clean out of existence? He was like a hipster puppy dog with zero people skills. Did I mention pathetic?

"Listen, you're right, I'm the worst. But I just want to make sure you know how much your mom loves you. You're pretty much all she ever talks about." I stared at him, kind of liking how easy it was to make him squirm. "That's all. Just thought you should know that."

"Thanks," I said, not sure if I really meant it. I kicked off and pedaled my bike for home.

CHAPTER 18

HOME

When I got to the trailer, the first thing I saw was Dad, leaning against the carport, talking into his phone. It was the real Dad, not the scary one who kept sinking deeper into his recliner cushions. The next thing I saw was Mom. She had one hand on Dad's arm and was listening in to his conversation. When she saw me, her eyes lit up, and I could see right away that she was really Mom. Pink hair, kind eyes, big smile.

"Mom!"

She ran over and pulled me into a hug, and then Dad was hugging me too. I could feel his wet face against my bare shoulders.

"Dad, what's wrong?" I said, pulling back.

He wiped his face quick with his sleeve. "Nothing, baby. We were worried about you, that's all. I thought you might be back for lunch, but it's been hours. I was just calling my friend Jimmy down at the police station. Hold on, let me call him back."

"You called the police?"

"We couldn't find you," Mom said, squeezing my shoulders tight. I'm not gonna lie, all that hugging was pretty great. Here I'd thought my life was over, but it sure didn't feel that way. Dad called Jimmy, and then we all three hugged some more. I might have even teared up, a little.

It was just so good to be back home after everything that had happened. And it was good to have Mom and Dad back the way they should be.

"I talked to Gavin," I said as we started to head inside. The words kind of spilled out, and Mom and Dad exchanged a look.

"You did? When?" Mom blinked down at her phone. "Oh, that must have been why he was calling. I just ignored him when Dad thought you might be missing."

"You ignored him for me?"

"Of course." Mom's eyes teared up too, which never

happened. "You're my Junie Pie. You'll always be my Junie Pie. You're the most important person in the world to me." Yeah, we might have hugged some more, and the worst part was that I burst out in these ugly, throat-aching tears, even though I tried really hard not to. I guess I get that from Dad.

The crying went on for a while. Dad, of course, joined in, and Mom even let out a few quiet sniffles.

After that, we went inside, and Dad heated up some leftover pizza, since we still had four full boxes in the fridge. We sat on the couch, all three of us, with me in the middle. Dad drank a beer while Mom and I enjoyed our favorite, orange juice mixed with Mountain Dew. Oh, and we finally broke out the strawberry Twizzlers we'd gotten for Mom's surprise party.

While we were eating, Mom explained more about New York. It ended up that she wasn't planning to move away and never come back after all. She was leaving, but not forever. Her plan was to go to New York first to get everything set up at her new gallery space, and then come back in August to help me go school shopping and to generally hang out.

"But where will you live?" I asked, taking a long sip of fizzy orange juice. Already, I was starting to feel silly for making such a huge deal about the divorce. True, it was kind of the worst, but it wasn't the end of the world.

Mom rubbed my back, her usual quiet smile warming up her face. I'd never noticed before how much I loved that smile. "When I'm here, I'll stay in Bessy. That's what we call the silver submarine."

"And when you're there?" I said, knowing her answer, but still needing to hear it.

Mom kept on rubbing my back, but her smile faded a little. "Then I'll stay with Gavin. He has an apartment near the gallery."

"Are you getting married?" I looked over at Dad, who was busy studying the dirt under his fingernails.

"Not right away," Mom said. "Maybe never. We're just planning to take it one day at a time."

I tilted my glass, watching the last ice cube circle around in its watery prison. "Do you think you'll be happy?"

Mom opened her mouth, then closed it again. She looked over at Dad, but he kept his eyes firmly on his fingernails. "As long as I can still see you as much as possible, then yes. I think I will."

It wasn't perfect.

Mom would come home for a week every few months.

But my life wasn't over. Mom and Dad were still Mom and Dad, and we all loved each other. It wasn't exactly the same as before, but maybe it was good enough.

After pizza, Mom went home to Bessy, because I guess that was her real home now, and I tried my best to understand.

Dad asked if I wanted to stay up with him and watch bigfoot documentaries, but I said I was too tired. I scratched at my sweaty scalp under my hat, wondering if my hair had turned back to normal yet.

"Good night, Dad. Love you."

"Good night, honey pie."

"Oh, I almost forgot," Dad called me back. "You got mail." Dad grabbed an envelope from the hall table, aka the broken keyboard we used as a table, and handed it to me. It was from Calvin.

"Maybe it's a love letter," Dad said, wiggling his eyebrows.

"Dad! It so is not!"

"You know the Bigfoot Ball was tonight," Dad said, his lips twisting into a mischievous grin. "Who knows, baby. Maybe next year you and Calvin will be the ones dressing up all fancy."

"Dad!"

Back in my room, in bed this time, I sank down into my pillow and examined the letter. I turned on my lamp and held it up to the light. The envelope was too thick to see through. I remembered JUNIEPIE28's advice, but I wasn't sure I was ready to know what Calvin had written. What if it changed things? What if we started going out, like boyfriend and girlfriend, and then everything got ruined like it had with Mom and Dad? Was love even worth it if you knew that one day it might all go wrong?

Sigh.

I turned out the light and closed my eyes, resting the unopened envelope on my nightstand.

Dear June,

I don't know how to say this, so I thought I would write it down. Here it is. Ready? I like you. As in like-like you.

Is the world crashing down right now, or is it just me? If you don't like me back, it's totally fine. Really. You're my best friend, and you always will be. Hopefully. I just had to tell you. I wanted to do it in person, maybe at the ball, but yeah . . . in person is way too scary.

Anyway, I don't know what else to say. Except, if you don't like me, could we just never talk about this again? Like ever?

Love,
Calvin

CHAPTER 19

FLYING

Dad and I spent the whole afternoon decorating a new sign. We worked outside on the driveway so the house wouldn't be one big glitter bomb. Dad was not exactly a huge fan of glitter. He tried super hard not to get any on his clothes, but he so totally failed. By the time we were finished, we both looked like walking disco balls.

"Ain't she a beaut?" Dad said, standing back and admiring our WELCOME HOME sign.

"Sure is," I said, and she was. The most beautiful sign in the whole wide world. Sunlight shimmering off her rainbow-colored letters. Feathers doing little dances on the wind.

Once she was dry, I rolled her up nice and tight and put her in an old telescope case for safekeeping, and Dad helped me strap her to the back of Honey Pie. No way this sign would end up in a watery grave.

"Ready, baby?" Dad climbed on Honey Pie. She was all shined up and sparkly for the occasion. Twelve years and this motorcycle was finally set to hit the road. We'd already done the whole picture thing, me and Dad posing next to our super-old, but now super-shiny motorcycle. But seeing Dad sitting atop Honey Pie in his dusty boots and leather vest was a sight for the ages.

"Let's do this thing," I said, climbing on behind him. I may not have accomplished anything else from my vision board this year, like finding bigfoot or getting Mom and Dad back together, but at least I had Honey Pie.

If you've never ridden a motorcycle before, let me give you one piece of advice: Hold on tight. By the time we got to the airport, my hair was whipped up so good it looked like I'd passed through a tornado and a hurricane, and just barely lived to tell the tale.

My legs wobbled like taffy as I climbed off that bike

and returned to solid ground. I checked on the sign, happy to find that it was a-okay. Even being rolled up in that tiny case hadn't tarnished its beauty.

Dad and I claimed the airport's only bench, since we'd gotten there with plenty of time to spare. We unrolled the sign, just in case the plane decided to touch down early, and talked over all the things we would do once Mom arrived.

Dino Land was at the top of the list, since Mom would be staying just outside the gate, and she'd never actually been inside. Dad had read about this new art show opening in Tulsa, and he said we could drive up to check it out and maybe even stay the night. Mom would definitely be surprised when she saw Honey Pie up and running. Maybe she'd even go for a ride. And I couldn't wait to see Mom's new hair. I knew from her last email that she'd dyed it eggplant purple, but I had yet to see a picture. No doubt, it would be totally epic.

The sun dipped behind the trees as seven o'clock approached. I thought back to all the wild stuff that had happened over the summer. Finding out about Gavin. Trying to fix things, and failing. The shop, Mag and the tiger, Gomo. I couldn't help but smile thinking about that last one.

Already the memories had started to fade. I still remembered most of what had happened, but that week was like a

Polaroid picture that got left out in the rain. The impression was still there, but the edges were going blurry. Soon, there wouldn't be much left at all. Just a faint afterimage, a shadow of forgotten magic.

I wasn't the only one in town who was starting to forget. Stop someone on the street and ask if they've ever visited a magic junk shop or seen an angry gnome floating down Main Street. Nine times out of ten, they'll laugh in your face. Seriously. I've tried.

I smiled at the memory. My fingers went to the beaded bracelet on my wrist. The glass beads spelled out BIGFOOT LOVER with little red hearts on either side.

It was a gift. From Calvin.

Now, there's one person who was happy to forget about the magic. It ends up his magic spell, the one that had made an entire Girl Scout troop fall in love with him, had been meant for me. I know! So creepy, right?! Thankfully, he learned a big, mega-sized lesson, i.e., it's not cool to cast spells on your best friend! He apologized after . . . Like a lot.

And I never did tell him that I read the letter. But last week, we were riding our bikes out by the pond, searching for bigfoot, and it happened. Dad doesn't even know, but we were walking down a trail, the same one where I spotted Mag and Mr. Winkles, and Calvin tripped and I helped him up and . . . yeah, we sort of kissed.

Then he got me this bracelet, and I guess the rest is history. Sometimes, I wish I could talk to JUNIEPIE28 one last time, to ask about her boyfriend and whether or not it's really Calvin, but most of the time I think she's right. Life is better without spoilers. As much as we may want to control the future, or the people around us, for the most part we can't. And even if we can, it doesn't always work out the way we imagined.

Sometimes, life stinks and there's nothing we can do about it. But we keep going. And, hopefully, the stuff that seemed so terrible at first will start to feel a little less terrible over time. Then one day, we'll wake up and realize that everything turned out okay. Not perfect. Not just the way we imagined it. But at least okay.

As the sky turned a dark purple shot through with orange, the parking lot started filling up with trucks. People ambled over, carrying flowers and balloons and less-epic signs, joining us on the sidewalk, aka baggage claim. We all looked up as the silhouette of a plane broke through the clouds. Before the tires had even hit the ground, Dad and I got to our feet, sign in hand. All around us, people started clapping.

ACKNOWLEDGMENTS

First off, I would like to give a HUGE, MEGA-SIZED shout-out to my agent, Brianne Johnson. You go, you super-cool witchy rock star, you! And another GINORMOUS thank-you to my editor, Mallory Kass, and the entire crew over at Scholastic. You are the makers of dreams, my friends. All the hearts!

I'd also like to give a special, spooky shout-out to my friends over at spookymiddlegrade.com. You all are truly terrifying and delightful and, not even being dramatic here, a constant inspiration. And since I know how much we all love seeing our names in print, this one is for: S. A. Larsen, Samantha M. Clark, Victoria Piontek, Jonathan Rosen, David Neilsen, Tania del Rio, Lindsay Currie, Sarah Cannon, Kat Shepherd, Janet Fox, Cynthia Reeg, Angie Smibert, and Lisa Schmid!

Next on the list, I'm sending all the kissy-face emojis over to my SCBWI Oklahoma friends. You all are so totally awesome you're basically off the charts! I'm thinking of you: Regina Garvie, Gwendolyn Hooks, Jerry Bennett, Jessica Bennett, Patti Bennett, Tod Hardin, Jill Donaldson, Jeannie Hagy, Pati Hailey, Gaye Sanders, John Davidson, Jon Gilliland, Megan Cox, Mary Payne, Sandi Lawson, Megan Walvoord, Kara Mitchell, Alex Brodt, Sonia Gensler, Tammi Sauer, Anna Myers, and many, many more. And let's not forget about my other, just as fabulous writer friends, like Ashley Nixon (i.e., she of the world's coolest tattoo), Jennifer England-Burnside, Sean Burnside, and even the super-mysterious Fujii—you go write that children's book, you strange, strange soul.

And where would I be without all the amazing teachers and librarians out there who work so hard to put great books into the hands of readers? If I could design the world's spar-kliest, most beautiful sign in your honor, it would read, SUPERSTAR!

Don't even get me started on the total explosion of awe-someness that is all you FABULOUS readers out there. If I could throw you a party, it would involve a million puppies, barrels full of glitter, like ten rainbow dragons, and the world's most epic unicorn dance party. Just saying.

Finally, a MAMMOTH-sized thank-you to all the friends and family who have come out to support me over the years, that includes you, Mom. ☺ There are too many of you to name, but I'd like to send an extra-big kissy face to Aunt Christy, who organizes a family book signing for me every time I have a new release and texts whenever my books make the Oklahoma Best-sellers list. And a GIANT-sized thank-you to library warriors and overall amazing ladies Deb Smith-Cohen, Janine Perky, and Lynn Steele.

Thank you, thank you! In the words of June, you are all SO TOTALLY amazing!

ABOUT THE AUTHOR

Kim Ventrella is the author of *Skeleton Tree* and *Bone Hollow*, which *Kirkus Reviews* called an "emotional roller coaster tempered by a touch of magic." Her works explore difficult topics with big doses of humor, whimsy, and hope. Kim has held a variety of interesting jobs, including children's librarian, scare actor, Peace Corps volunteer, French instructor, and overnight staff person at a women's shelter, but her favorite job title is author. She lives in Oklahoma City with her dog and co-writer, Hera. Find out more at kimventrella.com or follow Kim on Twitter and Instagram at @KimVentrella.